The Butcher of Park Ex

and Other Semi-Truthful Tales

MIROLAND IMPRINT 22

Guernica Editions Inc. acknowledges the support
of the Canada Council for the Arts and the Ontario Arts Council.
The Ontario Arts Council is an agency of the Government of Ontario.
We acknowledge the financial support of the Government of Canada.

ANDREAS KESSARIS

The Butcher of Park Ex

and Other Semi-Truthful Tales

MiroLand
publishers

TORONTO • CHICAGO • BUFFALO • LANCASTER (U.K.)
2020

Connie McParland, series editor
Michael Mirolla, editor
Cover and interior design: Rafael Chimicatti
Cover photo: Peter Kessaris
Guernica Editions Inc.
287 Templemead Drive, Hamilton, ON L8W 2W4
2250 Military Road, Tonawanda, N.Y. 14150-6000 U.S.A.
www.guernicaeditions.com

Distributors:
Independent Publishers Group (IPG)
600 North Pulaski Road, Chicago IL 60624
University of Toronto Press Distribution,
5201 Dufferin Street, Toronto (ON), Canada M3H 5T8
Gazelle Book Services, White Cross Mills
High Town, Lancaster LA1 4XS U.K.

First edition.
Printed in Canada.

Legal Deposit—Third Quarter
Library of Congress Catalog Card Number: 2019949208
Library and Archives Canada Cataloguing in Publication
Title: The butcher of Park Ex & other semi-truthful tales / Andreas Kessaris.
Other titles: Butcher of Park Ex and other semi-truthful tales
Names: Kessaris, Andreas, author.
Description: First edition. | Series statement: MiroLand imprint ; 22 | Short stories.
Identifiers: Canadiana (print) 20190177748 | Canadiana (ebook) 20190177756
ISBN 9781771834919 (softcover) | ISBN 9781771834926 (EPUB)
ISBN 9781771834933 (Kindle)

Classification: LCC PS8621.E86 B88 2020 | DDC C813/.6—dc23

For Mom & Dad

CONTENTS

11   George Has a Purple Face

20   Mrs. Levine

26   The House on L'Acadie

32   Sunday Shopping

38   The Butcher of Park Ex

46   The Wad

50   The Monopoly

56   The Time I Did Not Meet
Pierre Elliott Trudeau

63   The Legend of Shitboy Monster

67   The Music Man

76   A Day at the Beach

84   Playing the Slots

89   The Seer

95   "Your Driver's License, You Infidel Dog!"

101   Sweet Judy Blue-Eye

109   Burned Bikers

113   A Souvenir of Letterman

122   The Red Velour Ropes

131   Superstition Is Not the Proper Means
of Getting Things Done

135   The Great White Hunter

140   The Merry Monk

145   20 lbs. of Flour

151   New Year's Day with a Dictator

158   The End ... and a New Beginning

170   *Acknowledgements*

171   *About the Author*

Author's Note

Although based on actual incidents, the following stories may contain embellishments, hyperbole is generously applied, some situations are amalgams or fictionalizations, a number of names have been changed, and certain characters are composites. Instances are often as the author remembers them, not necessarily as they factually transpired. This book was not written with the intention of hurting anyone.

GEORGE HAS A PURPLE FACE

My mother dressed me in my nicest shirt and bow tie that day; the same clothes I wore for church or a doctor's appointment, the concept behind which to this day I still have a tremendous amount of difficulty full comprehending: If I looked dapper would the doctor be less likely to diagnose something serious? You always had to undress at the doctor's anyway.

"Where are we going?" I asked.

"We are going to go register you for school in the fall. I can't believe you are already old enough for school! They are going to teach you to read and write, and you are going to make new friends! It's going to be fun!" She said all this in a tone that I mistook for joy; a joy that she's going get the house back to herself so she wouldn't have to look after me all day, which in and of itself was a full-time job. (My parents tried to put me in a nursey school on St. Roch and Durocher, but I didn't react well to that. It went so badly that Mom almost lost her job because she often stayed home with me when they couldn't handle me at daycare, finally finding relief when Mrs. Theofanos, a housewife who lived across the street with a son the same age as my brother, agreed to watch me when my mom was at work. Mrs. Theofanos was pregnant at the time, so her baby-sitting duties lasted until she gave birth a few months later, just long enough for me to go to school, which was required by law, so the teachers couldn't as easily disencumber themselves of me like the daycare workers did. I was going to be the school's problem now.) Later I realized it was more accurately a combination of pride and hope on my mother's part.

I was still unsure as to why I had to dress up. Was this like a job interview? Was there a chance they wouldn't take me if I was in tatters, or even just a little more casual?

The office in question was in the municipal building on the corner of Bloomfield and Ogilvy. It also housed the local fire department and a children's library. When we entered the small, cluttered room there were already several mothers present waiting to sign their kids up for the PSBGM. One was with a young girl in the process of getting registered, also dressed in her finest, so I guess my mother wasn't the only one to practice that sort of thing. The other was a boy with his mother and they were playing with a small ball, tossing it back and forth. When it was their turn to register, my mom decided that we should play with the ball now, despite the fact that I was not in the mood. I'm not sure why but Mom always felt the need to do exactly what every other mother and son did. I told her I had no interest, but she persisted, and threw the ball at me. I displayed my protest by refusing to catch the ball and letting it drop to the ground in front of me. She tried again, and once again I denied the spherical object's existence. Mom knew better than to bawl me out or smack me in an official, public place, but I could tell that she was getting plenty steamed. She shot me an angry glare, and I shot right back my "I can keep this up as long as you can" look. After a few more attempts she wisely acquiesced.

This did not escape the notice of The Clerk, a portly and stern-looking late-middle aged woman in a beige dress with a white sweater draped over she shoulders. Her greying hair was rolled up in a loose bun with a pair of pencils jammed in there for good measure. She was the kind of woman the Greeks would call *Anglaisas*, which is Greek for "English woman," not necessarily referring to someone from England, but meant more to apply to all W.A.S.P.S, as well as the Irish or anyone who spoke English at home. Greeks also referred to people like her as a *Xenos*, which means "alien" or "foreigner," something I found odd seeing as how in Quebec and Canada we were considered the "foreigners" by the descendants of the British and French establishment. When it was our turn The Clerk's eyes scrutinized me from over the rims of her black plastic-framed reading glasses.

"Your son doesn't seem normal," she said bluntly. "Has he been to the doctor?"

"Yes," my mother said enthusiastically, "he *eez djust* fine."

"Are you sure?" The Clerk asked again firmly.

Mom nodded nervously.

"Can I see his birth certificate? Is he vaccinated?"

Mom provided the necessary documents.

"Can he dress himself?"

Mom answered yes.

"We'll see," The Clerk said as she produced two white swatches of cloth, one with a button hole, the other with a button and handed it to me. I immediately buttoned it up before she asked me to and handed it straight back to her.

If that was all there is to school, I thought, *this should be a breeze!*

"Okay," The Clerk said with all the emotion of a Vulcan High Priestess, after completing the necessary forms. "We will mail you a letter in a few weeks telling you when and where he is to go to kindergarten."

I'll never forget the relieved look on my mom's face. When we left the office she grabbed my hand and we shuffled away swiftly as if making some kind of getaway. I had the peculiar feeling like we had just pulled some kind of fast one on the school board.

Months later as Mom dressed me for my first day of kindergarten she told me to watch out for myself in the schoolyard.

"Peter had a problem with an older boy once, who kept hitting *heem*. So the next day I sent *heem* to school in his heaviest shoes, and I told *heem* to kick the boy as hard as he could. He did and the boy never bother *heem* again. If anyone tries to hurt you, you punch *heem* as hard as you can in the nose or the teeth, *na vgasis emma*. [Loosely translates as 'to make him bleed.'] I promise he will not bother you again." She said this with a pleasant smile on her face as if she were telling me to be a good boy or listen to my teacher, which she never did. That was the only academic advice she ever gave me.

Was I going to a school or to a prison? Where the hell is she sending me? Why would anyone want to hurt me?

As a child I attended Barclay Elementary, part of the now-defunct Protestant School Board of Greater Montreal, or PSBGM. Constructed in 1930, the monstrous, robust three-storey brown-brick building on Wiseman between Ball and Jarry Avenues encompasses an entire city block in the heart of Park Extension.

Kindergarten was not as difficult as my mother had predicted. I liked my teachers, one an experienced veteran in her late-forties, the other much younger and likely on her first assignment. The former was a "Mrs.", the latter a "Miss" and both were W.A.S.P.s. They were pleasant and patient and for me that academic year passed without incident.

It was 1975 and the English/French dispute in Quebec was reaching a boiling point. The PSBGM English schools taught French in Kindergarten once a week for half an hour. The French teacher, Madame Sigeault, whom I referred to as "Madame Seagull" (not as a sign of disrespect; I actually thought that was her name … I said it to her face and she never corrected me), a no-nonsense, middle-aged blonde with thick glasses who always wore navy blue or black polyester pantsuits, showed up once a week. She never spoke so much as a word to the English teachers, who always seemed to greet her arrival with a low-level degree of snarky contempt.

Madame Sigeault would arrange all the students in a circle and teach us things like: "*Où est le crayon? Le Crayon est sur la table.*"

The French lessons were not like regular class, where we played learning games and sang educational songs; it was rather dry and coldly bureaucratic. She would teach us how to obey commands in French like stand up, sit down, raise your right foot, turn around; like doing an atonal "Hokey Pokey." There was no real fun to Madame Sigeault's method. I tried to change that one morning. She asked us all the stand up and raise both our hands. I immediately waved my arms frantically and exclaimed: "I surrender! I surrender!"

Madame Sigeault shot me a glare that the Gorgon Medusa would envy. And the rest of the class didn't laugh. It was the first time a joke I had made bombed in front of an audience. Sadly, it would not be the last.

Mrs. McTiernan was my Grade 1 teacher. She was grandmotherly, and likely a few years past retirement age; typical old relic common in PSBGM schools when I attended. She had been teaching for so long that she would probably have had to dangle a student by their ankles out a window before she could get fired. My brother Peter had had her as a teacher three years earlier, and she remembered him.

She seemed to like me, but I believe it was because her mind was slipping and she thought I was my brother. (It was not uncommon for her to refer to me as "Peter.") She even gave me the weekly responsibility of wheeling the school's decrepit black and white TV into the classroom and plugging it in every Friday to watch an educational program called *Readalong*, a half-hour children's show produced by TVOntario that aired in Montreal on CBC channel 6. The show was hosted by a talking boot and taught the pleasures of reading and storytelling. I don't know what genius came up with the idea of talking footwear or how it related to literacy, but for me it was often the highlight of the school week. Maybe the show was financed by a grant from Bata or Aldo or something?

Mrs. McTiernan made us sing *O Canada* and salute the flag each day, something not done by any other Barclay teacher. She also made us pray in class first thing every morning, despite the fact that not everyone in multi-ethnic Barclay School was a Christian. In fact, the rarest thing one could discover at this "Protestant" school was an actual Protestant student, and a sizable portion of the teachers were Jewish. We had an occasional Catholic, usually an Italian or Portuguese kid whose parents must have gotten lost at registration time.

One of the few English Catholic schools in Park Ex at the time was Mother Seton Elementary, a small structure a few streets over on Bloomfield Avenue. It later became a French Language institution, and was renamed after Camille Laurin, the architect of Quebec's draconian language laws, which is a curious choice given its student body is and has always been almost entirely made up of the kind of ethnics, unwelcome by mainstream Quebec society, said laws were designed to assimilate; an irony lost on no one.

It wasn't a moment of silent prayer either. No, Mrs. McTiernan wrote it on the blackboard the first day of class and we had to memorize it. I went along with it because it was Grade 1 and I didn't know any better. My father told me to listen to my teacher, and even if I did tell on her, my moderately religious mother would not have complained because, as I found out later, her former one-room school in Greece also had prayers every morning, and truth be known she was not sophisticated enough to understand the concept of civil liberties and freedom of choice.

My father, on the other hand, was a politically active atheist who once told me that he stopped going to church the moment he was big enough to run away from his mother on Sunday mornings, and would never again for fear of bursting into flames upon entering any house of worship, and I realize now he would have gone totally ape-shit had he found out what Mrs. McTiernan was making us do. I don't know if any of the non-Christian kids told their parents about the prayers. Barclay was made up almost exclusively of immigrants or the children of immigrants who'd often fled political oppression in third-world dictatorships and were just grateful to be in

Canada where there were fewer death squads that hunted them on a regular basis, so they probably thought it prudent to avoid making waves. One of the kids was a Sikh named Tarsem, whom we all called "Tarzan," (similar to the Madame Sigeault incident it was not out of any desire to ridicule him but because we thought it was his actual name. The 60's TV series *Tarzan* starring Ron Ely was popular in re-runs at the time on Saturday afternoons). Tarsem prayed along with us and didn't complain once.

Although Mrs. McTiernan made the non-Christian students pray to Jesus, to be fair she was not a racist, and treated all students equally, whether good or bad. She was old-fashioned, and that included the way she disciplined the children. Mrs. McTiernan never struck any of the students, not like my first grade Saturday morning Greek School teacher, a psycho bitch who used to mercilessly beat her students with a yardstick if they misbehaved, had messy handwriting, or got an answer wrong. The first time she used it on me (the horrible, unforgivable offence I had perpetrated: I forgot one of my text-books at home!), I immediately informed on her to my parents. They took the maniac's side and said I probably deserved it (as a child I had numerous behaviour problems and was quite the handful for my parents and teach-ers alike, so they sympathized with her) and besides corporal punishment was practiced in every school in Greece, so they figured it was the same in Canada. But she really swung that yardstick hard! On one occasion a Greek School teacher beat my brother so bad, he was afraid to go back for weeks. I still find it odd that my father would have lost it had he discovered that we were made to pray or if we were ever taught religion, but beating and abusing us was to him somehow an acceptable practice. (I kept going to Greek school on Saturdays until the end of Grade 4 when I came home on the last day of classes tired of being bullied by the other kids for being so different, not uncommonly in class and on multiple occasions with the encouragement of the teachers, and declared in tears that I was not going back. Ever! That gave my brother the courage to do the same, and he stopped in Grade 7. To this day my father still derides us for quitting, but whenever he does, Peter and I form a united front and tell him we have no regrets. Not for a second.)

Humiliation was Mrs. McTiernan's preferred means of correcting stu-dents who made mistakes or whose behaviour deviated slightly. We were doing art one afternoon and our assignment was a self-portrait. As we were a group of six- or seven-year-olds, I don't understand why she expected us to be a bunch of Norman Rockwells. In my drawing I had committed the unforgivable sin of integrating my head and body as one unit. Mrs. McTiernan held it up to the class and said it made me look like Humpty-Dumpty, causing everyone to giggle. But luckily I was saved from further ridicule; before the nickname "Andreas Dumpty" could sink in Mrs. McTiernan snatched another unfortunate student's work and held it up before the whole class exclaiming: "Oh, Look everybody! George has a purple face! I didn't know your face was purple! It doesn't look purple to me!"

George P. was a thin, runty Greek kid with a disproportionally large head who resembled Alfred E. Neuman. He was in my kindergarten class a year earlier and was often picked on by bullies in the schoolyard. I hardly knew him and never gave him any grief myself, although I never stopped anyone from bothering him, either. His face was in fact not purple, but rather pale, and dotted with moles. I don't know why he coloured his visage purple, but there it was for all to see.

When Mrs. McTiernan said that line, I burst into uncontrollable and unstoppable laughter. It wasn't really George P. I was laughing at, but rather the way she delivered the line that I found hilarious. Most of the other students laughed initially, and then moved on. I of course had a terminal case of the giggles for the remainder of the day, annoying the rest of the children, many of whom could not get why I found it so hilarious, and pleaded for me to stop.

"Shut up! What's wrong with you!" they'd say. "It's not *that* funny!"

It especially irked George P.

My comeuppance came days later during an in-class reading competition. Mrs. McTiernan divided us into two teams of equal size. We formed twin lines down the centre of the room. She had prepared dozens of flashcards with simple words like "dog" or "house." Two students (one from each side) would approach her and she would reveal the word. The first child to say it correctly scored a point for their team. (Mrs. McTiernan's young teacher's aide kept score.) If you got it wrong, you were eliminated and had to stand at the back of the class. The team with the most points by lunchtime would be declared the winner.

I fancied myself rather bright and the superior intellect at the time and thought this would be my chance to shine and win the game for my team, proving to Mrs. McTiernan and my dimwitted moron classmates just how great I was. Beforehand I even bragged about how I planned to dominate the match and lead our team to victory.

So the game began, and I was near the front of the line. Finally it was my turn, and I knew I would get it because I was up against the purple-faced punk. Certainly I was smarter than him. I was brimming with over-confidence. Mrs. McTiernan held up a flash card which read "open" and I, for some reason, exclaimed "people!" I'll never forget the surprised, disappointed, almost personally offended look on her face.

"No, Andreas, that's wrong. What is the word, George?"

"Open," he announced confidently, with an impish grin that said: *My turn to laugh at you, motherfucker!*

I was the first person eliminated; soon followed by some of my less talented classmates, like the kid who ate paste, and the boy whose nose was always runny; a group that eventually included George P. To his credit he at least lasted longer than I did. So there I stood in the back with all the dumb kids. When the competition was over Mrs. McTiernan cruelly ridiculed us in front of the rest of the class, telling us to turn and face the window and hang our heads in shame. "I don't want to look at you! I'm ashamed of you all … I don't want to see your faces!" she said. On top of everything else my team lost, with me, the self-proclaimed superstar, tripping at the starting gate and falling flat on my face.

"I thought you said you were smart," one of the other students on my team said to me. "You're not smart at all!"

I felt so bad I couldn't reply.

With all her faults, I must confess Mrs. McTiernan did care about the children, just in an out-dated way. I think of the times when during school shootings teachers sacrifice their lives to save the students, and I have no doubt Mrs. McTiernan would have been the first take a bullet for us in such a crisis. It was just a matter of her antiquated mentality towards punishment and reward. And she taught me how to read and write, and I'll never forget that, or confuse "open" and "people" again.

Before I was finished with elementary school Mrs. McTiernan retired and I never saw or heard from her again. I still occasionally pass the old place while bike riding. The PSBGM is now defunct; Barclay's become a French-language educational institution and part of a new, different school board. They built a huge annex at the back, which to their credit sort of matches the rest of the building. The students are still immigrants or the children of immigrants, this time mostly from Asia, the Caribbean, Africa, or the Middle East. The ancient, wood-framed windows (so antiquated that we needed a pole with a hook on the end to open and close the top part when I attended Barclay) were replaced with more modern aluminum frames, but otherwise it still looks pretty much the same.

They painted a small mural on an outside wall explaining to kids how to settle disputes without violence. It makes me think about how education has changed over time. And how did my generation survive this?

MRS. LEVINE

I was raised in a culture that values strict, uncompromising adherence to the dogma of politeness and etiquette at any cost. Parents and schoolteachers bombarded us with the rules of proper manners, like never speak unless spoken to, never interrupt an adult, never contradict an adult, never say bad things about an adult no matter how truthful, never disobey an adult, never point out any adult's faults or misbehaviours, never refuse an adult any request, never stop an adult from doing whatever they want to you, etc., as if they were commandments carved in granite by an infallible deity.

Your worth as a human being was judged by how well you followed those rules, and if you broke one or even slightly deviated from their path, no one would take your side and you were labelled "naughty" or "impolite" and thrust out of regular society, scarring your family with a shame that would last for generations.

When I objected to that, my father promptly took whatever side was opposite mine and told me what I was doing was improper, as though I were still a child and debate on the matter was out of the question.

In my early teens my father's childhood friend from the old country, a hopeless, low-life alcoholic bum auto mechanic named Argethis, whom I called "*Archidias*" (Greek for testicles), came back to town after having abandoned his wife and kids to run off to the U.S. with his girlfriend. (The desertion in question transpired before I was born; and somehow *Archidias* was surprised when his family was a little lukewarm to his reappearance.) When she heard he returned my mother rolled her eyes and growled "*efto to katharmas!*" [Loosely translates as 'that dirtbag.']

Whenever I was alone with him and my father, *Archidias* would say things to me like: "You are the laziest kid I've ever known." Or: "You are a real loser, you know that?" Right in front of my dad, who seemed oblivious.

Once I shot back with: "Oh, yeah, you old drunk, why don't you run out on your wife and kids with some bimbo again –"

"*Stamata efto!*" my father said. "*Ama liess efta pragmata xena alimono sou!*" [Loosely translates to 'stop that!' and 'don't ever say anything like that again or else!']

Now he says something!

Dad never once backed me up or defended me to that souse.

Long ago my parents' limits were tested by the most unlikely source. It all began when I was five years old, and they were preparing for a caller. I paid little attention to our guest, choosing instead to play in our basement with my brother. After she left, my parents excitedly announced that we were soon to be the proud owners of a brand new set of encyclopaedias.

It was costly, especially for our family, but they believed it to be a wise investment. And that it was! My brother and I took to the books with eager curiosity and a voracious desire to learn.

They became my pre-internet reference source as well as my refuge. Whenever someone said something I was ignorant about, or I heard a person on the radio or TV mention anything unfamiliar, I would immediately make for our mini-library to look it up, and continued to do so until the internet and Google came along. Sometimes I would simply crack open a volume at random and start reading for the hell of it. When I didn't have many friends, I wasn't lonely because the encyclopaedias were there for me; they never judged me or lost their patience with me, and they always told me the truth. (Or at least a relatively fair version of thereof.) While most people look back on their childhood and wistfully recount reading *Green Eggs and Ham* or *Curious George,* the books of my youth were *The World Book Encyclopedia* and *Childcraft.*

I recall the day they arrived: hard-cover books carefully wrapped in construction paper and packed in individual white cardboard boxes with a pull tab for easy opening. To house them my parents had acquired an inexpensive but elegant-looking (from a distance) pressed-wood bookcase with sliding glass doors and gaudy plastic mouldings glued to the top. The set fit perfectly. The exquisitely bound tomes came with a massive, two-volume dictionary and an atlas. But, unknown to us at the time, they also came with something else: Mrs. Levine.

Mrs. Levine, the person who sold us the set, was a recently widowed retiree who took up the job on a part time basis to give her a *raison d'être*. Destiny brought her into our lives as one of my father's taxi fares.

The first time Mrs. Levine showed up unannounced was a few days after we took delivery. She said she came by as a follow-up to see if we liked our purchase, and was pleased to notice my brother and me leafing through them. My mother invited her, out of politeness of course, to stay and have a coffee and that soon turned into dinner. By my bedtime Mrs. Levine was still there, droning on about some damned thing or another in our living room. I have no idea at what hour she actually left, but I was surprised when she wasn't there the next morning; I fully expected her to still be on the couch, endlessly babbling.

It wasn't too long before Mrs. Levine popped in for a second time, and for a second time overstayed her welcome. And then again.

Back then my family was the hub of activity for our social group. My parents were like the Zelda and F. Scott Fitzgerald of working-class, Park Ex Greeks. Our cousins, uncles, aunts and other relatives congregated at our place most Fridays and Saturdays, primarily because we were always well-stocked with Molson Brador beer. My father was also very active in politics; it was not uncommon to find his nose buried in books with titles that translated in English to something like *Capitalism? Ha! You Make Me Laugh!*, so we had the bearded black-beret-with-red-star-wearing Ché Guevara wannabe clique as well. Dad organized multiple protest marches and rallies, including a march against the Vietnam War that started on Park Avenue and ended at the U.S. Consulate, then located on Bleury Street. (I was about three at the time, and fought the power from my father's shoulders that day.)

When Mrs. Levine dropped by unexpectedly, it was surreal watching an elderly, prim and proper, daintily-dressed, blond-haired blue-eyed *Anglaisas* navigate that crowd, oblivious to her square peg status. Everyone was scratching their heads as to who this person was and what she was doing there, leaving my parents to stumble through awkward, hasty explanations when she was out of earshot.

I did not relish my parents' social lifestyle. In those days, especially when company was over, I would wear a plastic Lone Ranger-like mask around the house, and skulk around with my head down trying to avoid eye contact, or any contact for that matter, with our aforementioned radical guests and their often annoying children, and try to do my own thing which usually entailed reading something. I did this until my father had had enough and angrily ripped the mask off my face and tore it in two right before me and everyone else.

Mrs. Levine once saw me with the mask on, crouched in a corner with my nose in a book just wanting to be left alone, and remarked that I was a "little devil," which my mom, who was filled with old-world superstitions, saw as taboo: It was absolutely verboten to speak like that for it would bring bad luck on the house and evoke The Evil One to claim my youthful, innocent soul! But she did not object out loud because it would have been improper to point that out to company. So I guess in my mom's reality my possible eternal damnation was less of a priority than offending an interloper.

Mrs. Levine started showing up for holidays. During one such visit, she announced that she had just adopted a dog, and insisted that come over to her house to see the pooch. My parents, not wanting to be discourteous, accepted the invitation, sternly warning my brother and me to behave properly and not spend all the time with her new pet.

Her dog reminded me of Toto from the *Wizard of Oz*. He jumped around a lot and yipped annoyingly. Mrs. Levine explained that whenever he got too frisky she would tap him with a rolled up magazine, and he would behave.

Did she do the same with her husband when he was alive? I pondered.

Mrs. Levine had a nice, middle-class home in Outremont. Her empty nest was clean but way too large for one person, and like her it had an aura of quiet, sad loneliness. She decorated her abode with photos of her late husband, daughters and grandchildren, and spoke of how she did not get to see them enough since they had all moved away. She prattled on about her maladies and a trip she took to Cuba, occasionally going so far as to let Mom or Dad get a word in edgewise. She served coffee, milk and cookies, and we stayed until it got dark outside. Our exit from there was more like an escape, with Mrs. Levine continually insisting we remain just a little longer.

We hoped that would be the last time we'd have to see her, but sure enough she kept finding reasons to pop in even after we moved to Stuart Avenue without telling her. (We had updated our encyclopaedias and those jerks probably finked on us.) Years went by. Eventually her dog broke its leg and had to be euthanized. (I personally believe it was a suicide.) After that the visits became more frequent. By then she was no longer selling encyclopaedias and perhaps hanging out with our family was her new career.

One gloomy Saturday afternoon when my father was out working and my brother was at a friend's house, I stayed home with Mom, who was curled up on the sofa-bed in our living room with a serious case of the flu. The sun had just set and the house was eerily dark, except for the dull, orange glow of our wood-grain Zenith System 3 console television, which as usual was on whether or not there was something worth watching. (I always found it odd that I hadn't heard of or seen a System 1 or 2, and whenever I inquired as to what exactly the 3 systems in question were, no one could give me a satisfactory response.)

The doorbell unexpectedly rang. I answered it. It was Mrs. Levine.

"Look at you, Peter, you have grown so much you are becoming a young man!" she said.

"Um, I'm Andreas."

"Of course you are," she said.

She came upstairs and went straight to my ailing mother.

"My, I didn't know you had a hide-a-bed! Isn't that nice, someone could stay over –"

I will never forget what happened next: my mother, who tried in vain to teach me all the proper tenets of socially acceptable behaviour and how they must be obeyed, no matter how ridiculous, inane, self-defeating or inconvenient; my mother, who put her cold, hard, heartless rubber-soled slipper to my backside with determination whenever I committed even a minor faux pas, which I seemed to do just about every time I interacted with another human being; my mother, who would die of embarrassment whenever my father recounted one of his many public thoughtless, crude, vulgar anecdotes; she gathered whatever strength influenza could not expunge from her weakened body and said: "Please Mrs. Levine, I can't today. *Please leave, Mrs. Levine,*" in a sad whimper not unlike that of a scolded canine.

Mrs. Levine stood stunned for a moment. Then she continued: "That fold-out bed must be useful; when you have guests they could sleep over –"

"*Please,* I'm sick, I *djust* can't do *thees* today. *Please leave now! I can't! I djust can't!*" Mom broke in with a combination of anger, desperation and frustration that I had never seen her use before on someone who wasn't a family member.

Mrs. Levine didn't say another word. She just calmly turned around and left.

Not long ago Mom moved to a senior's residence. There wasn't enough room in her new apartment for everything, so the obsolete encyclopaedias, along with many other furniture items and wall-hangings, had to go; my childhood was loaded into a recycling bin that day. With the exception of the glass doors, the old bookcase had held up well despite its poor quality. We left it out on the curb, empty for anyone who wanted to claim it. It disappeared within minutes. All that remains of the original set are the dictionaries and the atlas. They sit now on my overcrowded bookshelf like the ruins of a once magnificent temple.

And Mrs. Levine? We never saw or heard from her again. Among my family she became a forbidden subject; her name was never again to be uttered, lest she reappear. Occasionally I'd wonder if we were the only family she targeted, and if so why did she choose us? Was she angry or hurt by what had transpired? Did she ever think about us again? Did she miss us?

THE HOUSE ON L'ACADIE

When I was growing up my family never owned a home. We usually rented the top floor of a Park Extension row house duplex. When I was five we moved from such a dwelling on Birnam Street after residing there briefly. My parents didn't get along with the Boss (Park Ex'ers in those days always referred to their landlords as their "Boss." I'm not sure why. Perhaps it goes back to the old country where the rural Landlord was also sort of the farmer tenants' employer), a man I thought was named "Mooney" because my father constantly referred to him as "*toh moo-nee!*" when he wasn't around – I was ignorant at the time of what that word meant – until one day I called him Mr. Mooney right in front of my parents, who immediately started laughing and blushing. Fortunately, he was not Greek and had no idea I had just called him 'Mr. cunt!'

My mother worked at the time in a sweat shop for a low-end children's clothing manufacturer located in a factory on the corner of Park Avenue and Jean Talon Street. One day she came home and excitedly told my brother and me about new t-shirts they were making with original six hockey teams on them. Mom asked us which ones we wanted. It was 1974 and the biggest hockey player in the world at the time was Bobby Orr, so I said Boston. My brother chose Montreal. A few days later she came home with our choices. I proudly wore my black and gold Bruins shirt everywhere, including one time a few weeks later when I went with my dad to pick her up at work. We were early, and I knew what floor she worked on, so Dad let me go into the building to see her. When I showed up in the workshop, Mom died a thousand deaths. She quickly got up, grabbed me by the arm, and aggressively pulled me out of the room post haste.

"Go back to your father!" she yelled. "*Tora! Grigora! Exo!*" ['Now! Quickly! Out!']

I ran back to Dad in tears. When Mom came down a few minutes later, she furiously berated him for letting me go to her workplace wearing that shirt. Turns out she stole them.

While still living on Birnam, Mom and Dad invested in an industrial sewing machine manufactured by a company called Juki. It even came with a set of tools for maintenance, all labelled "Juki." At the time I thought that was cool. Mom was tired of working in the sweat shop and decided to go indie and do piecework at home for various clothiers as well as other seamstress gigs from local drycleaners and people around the neighbourhood.

On the day the massive machine was delivered and assembled, Mom proudly displayed it to my brother and me. She even let us have a go at it. Peter sat in the chair, carefully applied pressure on the foot pedal, and slowly stitched together two old rags. Then it was my turn. I sat down and immediately floored the pedal, sewing my index and middle finger together. Mom wouldn't let me near the machine again after that.

We found a new place to live on L'Acadie Boulevard between Ball and Jarry Avenues that was owned by one of my mother's former employers. It was an actual house for once; completely detached, simple and modest but with a basement, driveway, garage, and a backyard we didn't have to share with anyone else. What's more for the first time we would be living on the ground floor. There were two small rental units above us, but they were single bedroom bachelors and we rarely saw the transients who resided there.

The front door faced L'Acadie Boulevard and the hedge-lined Berlin Wall-style border fence that separated the Town of Mont-Royal – one of the Island of Montreal's richest municipalities (often referred to by locals as "The Town") – from Park Extension, one of its most economically disadvantaged. From our front balcony we could see the rooftops of the upper-middle class split-level single-family dwellings that most immigrants aspire to, but few reach. The wall consisted of a green chain-link fence with a tall hedge on either side and had gates pedestrians could use to enter or exit TMR from either Ogilvy, St. Roch, Jarry or Liège Avenues; gates that were always locked by the paramilitary rent-a-cops called TMR Public Security every Halloween to ensure that children from our side in their cheap costumes bought at the Rockland Woolworth's didn't get any of the candy intended for the rich, white *Anglaisos* children and their fancier cowboy or fairy get-ups purchased at Rockland's The Bay department store.

Whenever there was any vandalism on the TMR side, the residents would always blame the Park Ex'ers, totally ignoring the fact that it was their own rotten teenagers who were the likely culprits. But when the gates weren't locked during the hot, humid Montreal summers we would venture into TMR and ride our bikes around the winding, pristine, soulless streets and hardly ever see anyone, especially children. I later found out that they were either away with their families at some country vacation home or ushered off to some kind of camp deep in the forest so their parents could have peace and quiet for themselves. It was as if the houses with their carefully manicured lawns were mere façades.

Greeks residing in Canada didn't send their kids to summer or day camps. Instead they went to Greece for July and August. The fathers usually worked sixteen-hour days at their respective restaurants, and they would send the wife and kids to the homeland for better beaches, a dryer climate, and a more laid-back lifestyle. And to get peace and quiet for themselves as well.

The house on L'Acadie bordered an unpaved alley that cut across from L'Acadie to Birnam Street where children could safely play, but when I first saw the property what captured my imagination was the large vacant lot on the opposite side. My first thoughts upon setting eyes on it were of how much fun it was going to be to frolic there every day of the summer. It was like having a park right next door. We moved in on the first of July. The next day I awoke to find a huge yellow back-hoe parked on the property. And the day after that workmen came with several dump trucks and dug up the entire property about ten feet deep. Apparently the reason the previous tenants bugged out and the rent was so affordable was that a three-storey apartment building was about to be erected there and they wanted to take off before it happened. My parents were, to put it mildly, slightly upset that they were not forewarned about the impending construction before signing the lease. So was I.

My brother and I made fast friends with a skinny, blonde-haired Italian kid from across the alley named Johnny T., who age-wise was exactly between us. We used to hang out, now and again, with other children who lived on the alley, but primarily it was just the three of us. And on weekends we'd mess around in the massive pit with other neighbourhood kids who could not resist the lure of a forbidden construction zone. It was fun playing in there, although quite dangerous. Some of the boys would throw tiny stones they would find at each other and often fights would erupt. I remember getting solidly nailed by one, but never saw the culprit. The younger set, myself included, needed help climbing out when it was time to go home for supper. Johnny T. and my brother would never hesitate to give me a hand up, but others were less fortunate and sometimes remained trapped until their parents came looking for them. Kids would continue to trespass even well after the foundation was poured and the flat-slab construct slowly took shape.

It was not long before a huge truck dropped off tons of various assorted lumber products like large plywood panels and a seemingly infinite number of two-by-fours. During the week the loud, aggravating construction would continue, but on weekends the site was unguarded, with large piles of scrap wood dumped in the rear. Peter, Johnny T. and I would creep onto the property and nab as much as we could carry and, using our respective parents' tools (Johnny T.'s father had a wide assortment of the best hammers, screwdrivers and saws), we'd fashion the discarded lumber into elaborate, well-built (considering we were children) play sets for our eagle-eye G.I. Joe's with Kung-Fu grip or our superhero action figures. At night we would store the architectural marvels beneath our spacious backyard patio.

Other young Park Ex denizens would sneak onto the site to steal what they could, or commit inexplicably senseless acts of vandalism like smashing the soda bottles the workers left behind, unaware that they could have returned them to the local *dépanneur* for the deposit. Sometimes the owner of the lot would show up and chase the intruders away with a baseball bat, and other times he would have security guards do the same with night sticks. Our little trio had long since stopped going there except to pilfer the occasional piece of timber required to complete Spider-man's motel or G.I. Joe's sauna or Batman's gazebo or whatever we were working on at the time.

On a rainy day late in the summer my brother and I slipped onto the site for an attractive plank of plywood we noticed on the discard pile. There was already a large gang of kids messing around and causing havoc in what was by then a skeletal cement frame with interior stairs of red diamond-plate steel. The Fuzz unexpectedly showed up and one and all scattered like rabbits. Some of the trespassers were corralled by Montreal's finest, but most adroitly gave them the slip, jumping fences and escaping through various backyards. My brother and I managed to get back into our home safely but there was one minor hitch: They'd seen us.

We trembled with fear as a police officer walked up the front steps and rang the doorbell. We thought for sure the cops were going to drag us away in handcuffs. My mother was home and well aware of what was going on. She knew that we "borrowed" construction materials from next door; hell, she encouraged us and praised our creativity and ingenuity. It didn't hurt either that the activity also kept us busy and out of her hair while she spent the better part of her day working in her sewing room.

My brother and I watched from the living room window as my mother talked to the officers on the sidewalk in front of our house for over twenty minutes. We could not make out what she was saying. Typical for her, she was animated but kept her cool, constantly smiling and being otherwise pleasant, and did not give them a chance to say anything. I'm not sure what it was about her, but my mother always knew how to get people to do what she wanted. If we went to a restaurant and there was a line-up to get in, she would ask to speak to the manager and aggressively say things like "we've been dining here for years" or "I know the chef's wife" and suddenly we would find ourselves at the best table.

Mom led the officers, who by now were joined by the construction boss and the owner of the soon-to-be apartment building, to the backyard and showed them all the things we built with their lumber.

"What's she doing?" Peter asked me. "Why is she showing them what we stole? Is she trying to get us into more trouble?"

We retreated to our room to await the inevitable. About five minutes later Mom came in and told us not to worry, the police had gone.

"What happened?" we asked.

"I told them that you were *djust* taking useless old pieces of wood and using them to make things for your toys so you can play with. I showed them what you made. They left you some more wood in the driveway if you promise not to go into the construction place again and I told them you would stay away from now on, so that's *eet*." Then, she threw up her hands and shot us her trademark wry smirk.

My brother and I looked out a window and saw a long two-by-four and some other used pieces of pressed-wood lumber in the driveway, which we quickly collected and stored for later.

We considered ourselves fortunate and never went onto the site again. Within a year the building was complete. The view from my bedroom window became a depressing brick wall that blocked all sunlight. Soon hapless people started moving into what was ultimately a poorly-made yellow tenement that to this day remains an eyesore in an area containing some of the more charming residences in Park Ex.

We lived on L'Acadie for two years before the house's proprietor sold it out from under us. My parents found a cheaper rental on Stuart Avenue; another second floor row house duplex, where we would end up living for over a decade.

It was a sad day for me when we left. I'll never forget the house on L'Acadie.

SUNDAY SHOPPING

A while ago my brother and I were driving past a shopping mall on Easter Sunday. It was odd seeing the parking lot completely empty.

"Y'know," Peter said, "kinda reminds me of the time before they had Sunday shopping."

"That's true," I said. "Like when we were kids."

Sunday shopping in Quebec is a relatively new thing. When we were young, the law strictly forbade Sunday shopping so that people would have no choice but to attend church.

In the '70's my family would sometimes visit the closed shopping malls. My father was a taxi driver who worked twelve-hour days. He had to work Saturdays, but Sundays were slow enough that he could take most of the day off and not miss any business. So on rainy, dreary afternoons when we didn't go to the park with our cousins or to the movies or do some other family activity, we would go to the closed malls for some window shopping, checking out things we could never afford. The commercial establishments in question often contained restaurants and certain other businesses like movie theatres and pharmacies that were not bound by out-dated religious laws, so their doors would be open even on the Sabbath. Every now and again – such as Easter-time – they would have petting zoos.

I was just a boy of six or seven, but I enjoyed it. We went mostly to either Les Galeries D'Anjou in the "Far East" or The Fairview Centre in Pointe-Claire on the West Island. Sometimes I would come across a really cool toy store and want to come back when it was open. I'd ask Mom or

Dad if we could, and they'd say yes, most likely just to shut me up, because they'd never bring me back on a business day.

That sort of family outing suited my dad just fine, because he was somewhat careful with a dollar. No, that's not quite right … more accurate to say my dad would squeeze a penny so hard that the little Queen Elizabeth II on it would scream: "Oww! Bloody hell!" What he liked best about those outings is that they didn't cost much. And he absolutely loved it when it didn't cost anything at all.

One day they opened an arcade at the Fairview Centre. My father especially hated places like that, likening them to the casinos his younger brother, a high-rolling gambler who lived in South Africa, would frequent. (Said brother died broke and alone.) To Dad they were nothing more than cheap thrills and a total waste of time and money. However, when my brother and I saw it, we begged him for some quarters. He eventually relented, and after we spent them, we went back and hit him up for more. When he refused, we would get angry and make a big enough fuss that one time our parents took us straight home. He was probably the one who lobbied the government to eventually pass a law banning those under eighteen from such businesses.

When we actually had to buy something and a visit to the mall was unavoidable, my father would run it like a military commando raid. First, he would scout out the location alone and find what we needed at a price he could live with. Then he would return with my mother, brother and me for the purchase. He wanted us in and out as quickly as possible, so no one would get hurt, and so we wouldn't see anything else we'd like to buy or another store we'd like to browse. My father was a pragmatist and communist who saw browsing as a superficial, bourgeois and contemptible activity. He could never understand why people would look at items in a store that were neither a necessity nor affordable. My mother, on the other hand, loved to look around, especially the expensive stuff, although I think she did it just to raise my father's blood pressure a few points.

I was so used to seeing the mall closed that being there during business hours became a totally different experience, like visiting some parallel universe. The mall was alive! Stores were bright and open, the walkways were full of people, and there was music playing, albeit soul-sucking elevator music.

There was one instance when we needed a new living room couch. For such items my father would stay away from department stores, where most people went at the time, because you could not bargain. And he dreaded the idea of handing over his hard-earned money to the *Anglaisis*. He found a furniture store on Park Avenue owned by some Greek guy that was recommended to him by a friend, the most appealing aspect of which was that the aforementioned owner was always willing to negotiate. Likely he started off with a price that was ridiculously high, and would be talked down to something more sensible, though he would still make a killing, and the customer would feel like they got a deal and saved face even if they knew they didn't really. My father was like that: It's not how much he paid, but how much he was able to get the other guy to compromise, so he could brag that he talked someone down and got a good deal, thus saving his manhood.

In the showroom we found a hideous but solidly built couch. It was a custom-made piece that was never picked up and on sale for a pretty decent amount. The only drawback: This was the mid-'70's and it was bright orange. The upholstery was made of a mutant orange-plastic carcinogen that was likely extruded in a Taiwanese factory by a James Bond movie-like villain evil industrialist. But for my father cost was king, so we were interested; and although it was already fairly low, and a good deal, for him it was still not quite low enough.

So we repaired to the furniture store owner's office to discuss how much we were willing to pay to take the monstrosity off his hands. The office was large and neat, with an oversized, finely-crafted oak desk that took up three-quarters of the room. But its most prominent feature was a gargantuan and grotesque mural of Christ's head and upper torso on the cross, with his arms stretched across several walls. The art was incredibly detailed, and included blood dripping down the sad, tortured face of Jesus. I sat in a chair directly below his right hand and was fixated on the bloody nail that pierced his palm.

Why would the furniture store owner do this to his office? Who was he trying to impress? Was he trying to intimidate us by saying: "I'm really religious, so bow before me! And pay too much for my furniture, like Our Lord intended!"

The haggling session soon escalated to an ugly shouting match as the two small, swarthy Greek men gesticulated and cursed each other until a final price was settled upon; a sum neither seemed pleased with. And as usual my father staunchly refused to pay for delivery.

"No way am I going to pay *efto toh, toh, toh, salababeech, facking-bastar* to do that! Never!" he'd proudly proclaim. "And give a tip to the *facking* delivery guy *djust* for doing *heez djob!*" A sentiment I found rather peculiar, because as a cab driver Dad accepted tips all the time.

Fortunately like I said it was the '70's, and cars back then were colossal. My dad owned a four-door 1974 Chevy Chevelle so monstrous that the U.S. Navy offered to buy it from him for use as an aircraft carrier. It was so mammoth that at one point while on a car-trip to Florida, my father, brother, my mom and I all sat on the bench-sized front seat with plenty of room left over. And the beast was fast: On that trip we followed a Corvette going almost 100 mph through three states. There we were, all four of us with no seat belts barrelling down the Interstate, and my father steering with only two fingers on the wheel, casually smoking one of his Export 'A' regulars with the other hand. All we needed was a minor slip, and that car would have been our discount mass-burial coffin. The motorized vehicle in question was also a former Sûreté du Québec cruiser that still had police markings when my father bought it. (*The Blues Brothers* later copied us.) He didn't want to pay to have it painted, opting instead to paint it himself using house paint and a vacuum cleaner on reverse. Miraculously he did a decent job, but the colour, a glistening green, annoyed my mom. My father had a preference for green because it was the official colour of *PASOK*, the left-wing socialist Greek political party he dedicated his life to supporting. (My father was a zealous supporter and organizer for *PASOK*; so much so that when its leader, Andreas Papandreou was exiled in the late 60's, Dad went around collecting $5 from every member of the Greek community he could find to bring Papandreou to Canada, who eventually settled in Toronto. When Papandreou was elected Prime Minister of Greece in 1981, my father was rewarded for his efforts with the offer of a job at the Greek embassy in Ottawa; a job he refused saying that what he did he did for patriotism and principle, and not for any personal gain. For my mother that was the last straw. She put up with him spending all his time for political causes in the hope that there would be a light at the end of the tunnel: A better life for the family. She divorced him a couple of years later.)

So it was up to me and my brother to help Dad load the couch into the trunk. Dad did most of the heavy lifting, though. While my father is almost comically short and stocky, in his prime he was very strong, conditioned from years of working on my Grandfather's farm; at the age of fifteen, Dad had his first paid job manually hauling loads of bricks to construction sites.

The car's trunk was spacious but the couch of course did not fit perfectly. About two-thirds of it stuck out the back.

"No problem," Dad said. He then shoved it as deep into the trunk as he could. "Okay, let's go!"

We objected and suggested he try and tie it with rope. It was balanced rather precariously. One bump on the road and ...

"Ahh, *eet eez* fine. Let's go!" Dad said as he threw up his arms.

My brother and I knelt on the backseat facing the rear window and gazed in horror at the cargo, worried it would fall out on the street. My father drove fast and weaved through the traffic like he always did as if he were unaware of the load we were carrying. The trunk lid bobbed up and down as he started and stopped, but we made it home safely.

"See! I told you!" he'd said.

Didn't we feel like idiots!

The three of us lugged it upstairs where it remained our main living room couch for more than a decade, with one slight change: The upholstery. When we would sit on the couch shirtless or in shorts, especially on warm days, the fabric would stick to us and otherwise irritate the skin. So after a year my mother saved enough to have it re-done with a friendlier green and gray flower-pattern textile.

When it was time to replace the couch, my mother asked me to help her carry it down the stairs to leave on the curb, but not before ordering me to take the big kitchen knife and slash the cushions. I found it a peculiar request and asked why we would do that if we were throwing it out.

Mom flew into a rage and said that she didn't want anyone else to have it for free. When I objected again she got the knife herself and when at that couch like a serial killer. And after we dumped it on the street, she sat on our second-floor balcony and kept an eye on it to ensure that no one took the couch but the city's sanitation workers. After about an hour I could hear her shouting something like: "Get away from that! Shoo! Shoo!" She rushed into the house and down the stairs so quickly I didn't get a chance to ask what was going on. After a few minutes she came back in and told me to gather any clothes that I had outgrown or didn't wear anymore.

"Why?" I asked.

"The family that *eez* taking the couch they are new to Canada. They are from Pakistan or something and they're poor and have *tsildren*! Let's *geev* them some clothes! Hurry, get your clothes!"

I was more than a little perplexed as to why she had a change of heart, and not only could someone take the couch for free, but they were also going to get the clothes off my back. Then I realized she probably just didn't want *Greeks* to take the couch. We gathered a small bundle of clothing and gave it to them in a black garbage bag, which they gratefully and humbly accepted.

Years later I was working at a mall managing a record store. On a rainy, morbid Sunday I closed alone and was hit with a haunting, *déjà vu* episode as I was leaving. I looked around the empty, unlit establishments and kiosks and saw no one. I stopped dead in my tracks and for a moment I was travelling back in time. I could see my brother jumping from bench to bench. My mom and dad walking together hand in hand. A reflection of me as a child, peering through the window of a darkened toy store with desirous eyes. It was a warm feeling like I had not experienced in years. I stood there for a few minutes, and just absorbed the surroundings. Then it slipped away into the dreary evening.

THE BUTCHER OF PARK EX

In the 1970's Pierre Elliott Trudeau was our Prime Minister, the Olympics were in town, the Habs were winning Stanley Cups, Montreal was the largest and most important city in Canada, and Park Extension was my home.

At the end of Park Avenue and nestled in between the Metropolitan Expressway on the north, Boulevard de l'Acadie on the west, and railroad tracks on the south and east is Park Ex with its endless row-houses, dilapidated tenements and crumbling apartment buildings; a haven where new arrivals to Canada first settle until they could afford to live somewhere better. It is so ethnically diverse that I would go so far as to wager that on each city block in Park Ex one can find residents originally from every continent except Australia and Antarctica. It is the most densely populated neighbourhood in Montreal, and among the poorest per capita urban areas in Canada. And it was during the '70's that the Hellenic Community's influence on that district was in its heyday, representing more than 50% of the population.

When I was little, every Thursday afternoon after school my mother and I would walk to the local grocery store on St. Roch Avenue; a modest establishment, not much larger than a *dépanneur*, but it had everything we needed. It was called the SPG Grocery because it was founded, owned and operated by three guys named Spiro, Peter and George; a proud trio of Greek immigrants who came to the new world to pursue their dream of eking out an existence while wearing long white coats and working twelve-hour days, seven days a week. Spiro and Peter ran the grocery part of the establishment, one of their teenaged sons did deliveries with a three-wheeled bike equipped with a huge basket on the front, and the meat counter at the back, right next to the slimy olive barrels, was the exclusive domain of George, the Butcher of Park Ex.

George the Butcher was a big, beefy guy with a grizzled, hard-bitten face that looked like it wore out several bodies. He had pale skin, soulless, empty, light blue eyes, sideburns, and long, blonde, thinning, heavily-greased, combed-back hair with greying temples. His meaty hands had kielbasa-sized fingers that were calloused, disfigured, scarred, and had several missing tips. And he was strong. I once saw the mighty Butcher of Park Ex carry two entire pig carcasses, one over his shoulder and one under his arm, from a delivery truck to his dark, cavernous meat locker, which somehow contained the slaughtered remains of every animal in creation hanging on a hook. If someone asked for a goat, with horns, teeth, eyes, tongue and hoofs still attached, he would disappear into the dark recesses of his dominion, eventually emerging with whatever the customer wanted, as if it were a gateway to another dimension. He utilized his heavy meat cleaver, cacophonous electric band-saw, and long butcher's knife with the skill of a surgeon and the subtlety of a lumberjack. It would take him only a few violent, blood-soaked, gory minutes of hacking, carving and slicing to reduce a heifer into thick red slabs of rib steak.

The meat counter was, oddly enough, where another form of brutality took place. It was where all the Greek housewives would congregate and engage in sparkling conversation, and by that I mean they would gossip about matters that were often inaccurate and exaggerated, and never a damn bit of their business.

My mom knew, or more precisely claimed to know, every Greek in Park Extension through what was then her analog version of Twitter. When Mom would arrive, a woman would usually already be there waiting for her warthog to be chopped into bits. Said woman would relate to my mother the latest horrific misfortune that allegedly befell some unfortunate sap in Park Ex. Then the gossiper would leave. While Mom waited for her order another woman would inevitably appear, and of course Mom took it upon herself to pass on the news, adding her own personal twist to the tale.

The poor butcher had to listen to a hundred different versions of the same story all day long, but he would never participate and didn't even seem to pay attention. In fact, I rarely heard him utter anything other than the occasional grunt when wrestling a difficult steer from a meat hook or Greek profanity when he'd accidentally amputate another of his fingertips while dismembering a walrus. The customer would simply tell The Butcher what they wanted, he'd nod ever so slightly to show that he understood, and went about the task of preparing the order and wrapping it up in butcher paper, which he'd then weigh and price with a magic marker. No patron ever dared barter for a better price or ask him to trim of the fat from a steak, probably out of fear they'd end up in the meat locker hanging next to the zebra.

It never bothered me in the least that Mom would occupy her time with relaying erroneous stories about other people. What annoyed me was Mom's insistence that she impart the vital piece of information to me during the walk home. She'd usually begin by asking if I had ever heard of a particular person.

"Do you know Tasso Papathanasios?"

"No," I'd answer, knowing that something horrible must've befallen that unlucky soul.

"You have to know him. He goes to Barclay. He has a brother named Petros who *eez* your age!" she'd insist, unaware that eight-year-olds do not often exchange the same meaningless social information as adults. My main concern at that age was how to become Han Solo, not whose parents are divorcing or whose cousin was torn apart by wild dogs. Also, Barclay Elementary was at its operational peak with over one thousand students, and all the boys were named either Tasso, John, George, Nick, Stavros or Christos, and everyone was everyone else's relative. It was entirely possible that I'd be familiar with that person's face and not be acquainted with the specific individual to whom she was referring, but his name didn't ring a bell.

"Anyways," she'd continue, because for whatever reason she felt obliged to continue no matter what, "he was riding *heez* bicycle the other day, and *heet* a bump or something, and fell off, and cut *heez* leg badly. It got infected and they had to amputate!"

"So what?" I'd ask. "Why are you telling me this? I said I don't know this kid."

"That poor boy lost *heez* leg! Don't you care?"

"What do you want from me? You want me to cry? What good does this do me?"

"It's *djust* a lesson for you to be more careful on your bicycle. You know I don't want you to get hurt."

This was the same woman who would mercilessly beat me with a hard, rubber slipper when I'd misbehave, or if she was angry at someone else and I was the only person within arm's reach, so I had to pay the price, and suddenly she was concerned for my wellbeing?

To be fair to my mother, what was tantamount to child abuse was a very common practice among Greek immigrants at that time. If any child of a Greek ever acted out, the parents' instinctive reaction was to strike said child as hard as they could, and in public if necessary, although most were a little more discreet. In fact, a periodical called *Child Abuse Monthly* was published in Greece. It contained articles about newer, better ways to abuse children. One of their pieces was entitled **CRUCIFYING YOUR CHILD: TOO FAR OR NOR FAR ENOUGH?** Greeks went beyond corporal punishment, usually achieving the level of Sergeant; and not the regular three-stripe sergeant, either. I'm talking the kind of sergeant with the three bottom stripes and the little gold star in the middle; something more along the lines of Sergeant *Major* Punishment. Slippers, wooden spoons, coat hangers and belts where often their weapons of choice.

But then few things about Greek culture made sense to me. When I was twenty my mother remarried, and one day I told her and her new husband about a recent incident that occurred to my friend The Weasel's older brother Sam: He had lent his car to a friend, who promptly wrecked the motorized vehicle in question without insurance (he was unhurt), leaving Sam without a ride and less one friendship.

"You see," my mother's husband firmly stated, "you should never lend out the *munneez*, the *woo-manz*, or the car to your friends! Never!"

While I did not care for him thinking of my mother as property, I was glad to see that he at least regarded her more highly than his car.

Whenever a Greek man uses the term "the *woo-manz*" in a sentence one should brace themselves for the worst thing they can possibly hear. Once when my mother caught wind that her sister, at the time six months pregnant, expecting for the third time in five years, had to haul a mammoth drum of olive oil (for reasons that to this day I still have a tremendous amount of difficulty fully comprehending, Greeks always feel compelled to have a stockpile of olive oil in their pantry, basement, or hidden somewhere in their homes … when I once asked my father if I could store my winter tires in the storage locker he had in the basement of his condo, he told me I couldn't because it was already filled to the top with olive oil barrels. When I asked why an eighty-year-old man required a forty-year supply, all he could say is that he was an optimist. Serves me right for asking), up six flights of stairs without help from her spouse, she confronted her brother-in-law to demand why.

"That *eez* the *djob* for the *woo-manz!*" was his only reply.

The next day at school I searched the playground for a kid with a wooden leg or crutches. I even asked around a bit, but no one knew what I was talking about.

Did one of the busybodies just make the whole thing up? Was the story changed from woman to woman until embellished beyond recognition? Did Mom hear it wrong? I never found out, although she continued to insist on its accuracy.

My mother, like most Greek women, was constantly exaggerating and overreacting to situations. When my brother Peter was seven or eight years old, he thought he was Evel Knievel and decided to build a ramp out of pilfered construction plywood and bricks in order to jump with his bike over a large puddle in the lane adjacent to our house. He of course only managed to injure himself, badly skinning his knees and elbows. My mother's first reaction was to panic as though he were scarred for life, and this was the greatest tragedy that had befallen any family in the history of humanity. Then she carefully cleaned his wounds with a disgusting brand of iodine that coloured his arms and legs red for days. To teach him a somewhat ironic lesson she then beat him with her slipper. A lot of good it did: The next day, "Perilous Pete" tried the jump again, and was inexplicably surprised when unsuccessful for a second time.

"Mom! A mosquito bit me!" I'd say.

"Oh good God, no! The humanity! Now you are scarred for the life!" she'd shriek.

"Mom! The mail is late!"

"Call a doctor! I'm having *tsest* pains!" she'd cry.

She's been having a heart attack a day since the late seventies.

My dad, on the other hand, was like a Bruce Willis or Arnold Schwarzenegger character in an action movie, in that he could shrug off anything. If a building were to collapse on Dad, he would miraculously emerge from the rubble unscathed, shake away the dust, and keep going without getting the slightest bit upset.

My father has so far survived a gunshot wound, fistfights, multiple car accidents, a stabbing, two hernia operations, haemorrhoids, major back surgery, and worst of all, three marriages.

Dad's technique for enduring the aforementioned was to simply throw up his hands and exclaim: "Ahh!" as if it were nothing.

"Dad! A shark just bit off your legs!"

He'd throw up his hands and say: "Ahh!"

"Dad! A meteor is about to strike the Earth and wipe out all of humanity!"

He'd throw up his hands and say: "Ahh!"

On another trip to the butcher counter Mom was horrified to discover that wolves were living in Montreal. This was, of course, based in fact: Coyotes were discovered in Bois-de-Liesse Park, a West-End mini-forest. They likely made their way there via a nearby railroad track, but the way Mom described it to me, they "came by the train," to which my eight-year-old imagination ran wild. I pictured the coyotes in question jumping boxcars like hobos or riding on the rails like passengers with tickets. Either way my mom feared they were now roaming Park Ex like a street gang.

Mom continued to regale me with her tales from the meat counter even after I was older and stopped accompanying her to the grocery store. One time she told me of a waiter's sad fate. Apparently he ran out into the street after a dine-and-dash deadbeat, and was subsequently hit by a car and killed. Strangely enough, I never heard a thing about that incident in the media.

"C'mon Ma," I said. "I told you I really don't want to hear any more of those dumb stories!"

"But he had a wife and five *tsildren*!"

"Well, he should've kept his pants on!" I retorted.

Much to my surprise, she laughed at that.

For a long time I never understood why Mom was so obsessed with telling me about the misadventures of others. And it wasn't just me, either. I arose once to the faint sound of her telling the dog about the man down the street who regained consciousness one morning in a bathtub full of ice without his pancreas after a night of partying with a strange, non-Greek woman he should not have trusted. Another time I caught Mom alerting her budgies to the dangers of not returning chain letters.

That's when I finally got it: For Mom, it wasn't about the family trampled to death at Granby Zoo by a rogue hippopotamus; it was about talking. She just enjoyed engaging others in conversation.

Soon my brother and I became adults and moved out. Mom retired and with extra time on her hands, became more active in the community and church, and eventually started hanging around with a group of women her age. She started her own a part-time business taking elderly Greek women, most of whom were widowed, to doctor appointments. Because they were traditional housewives who hadn't worked outside the house, they never learned English or French, so Mom would act as translator. They would pay her a few dollars for her service, or buy her lunch. If they were poor Mom would do it for free.

It eventually became time to pass the neighbourhood on to the next group of immigrants. Slowly Park Extension went from being occupied by the Hellenic Community to South Asian domination. Soon enough Spiro, Peter and George retired, and the grocery was sold to three brothers from Bangladesh conveniently named Sabir, Parvez and Gohar. The few remaining old-school Greek women in Park Ex stopped shopping at the SPG in favour of the new huge chain grocery store on Hutchinson and Jean-Talon, which has lunch tables set up near the entrance where they congregate and gossip.

The Habs are no longer winning cups, the Olympics are over, Toronto has overtaken Montreal as Canada's number one city (a victory I consider to be by default), but a Trudeau once again became Prime Minister.

I found myself recently at my mother's apartment in a Park Ex seniors' residence. As my brother was preparing our lunch, I sat at the dinner table with Mom and my teenaged nephew, who had recently adopted a miniature Doberman that he allowed to sleep in his bed with him under the covers.

"Don't do that, Anthony!" Mom, still spinning those yarns, said. She quickly related a story of how, when she was a young girl, a boy in her village was playing with the family's pig, and the animal became agitated and bit off the young lad's penis.

"I used to let Isabella sleep on my bed all the time," I said, "and there were never any problems. In fact, remember our cats, like the tabby Henry we used to have? He used to sleep on my bed all the time! Don't tell him bullshit like that!"

"*Alithea le-oh!*" ['I'm telling the truth'] she said.

"Oh yeah!?! What was the boy's name, then?" I said while eating potato chips out of a large, yellow, family-sized bag.

"Andreas, stop talking with your mouth full of chips, especially over the open bag, that's disgusting! Those chips are for all of us, y'know?" Peter said.

"Ohh," I replied, "you have a problem with me eating chips but a bull-shit urban legend story about a rabid hog biting off someone's dick! That's okay with you?"

That shut him.

I'm still not sure exactly why my mom sat on a story like that until she was well into her 80's. If I saw or heard about a hog chewing off someone's shlong, that would be the first thing I told anyone; hell, I would talk about it non-stop.

Not long ago I went to the SPG for a litre of milk and a lotto ticket. The current owners renamed the store, and even though the setup inside was essentially the same, it felt weird. Sure, the old meat counter was still there, but alas, with the Greek women gone nevermore will pathetic yarns of woe and misfortune be spun before the Butcher of Park Ex.

THE WAD

One Halloween my partner at the time sent me to a large produce store in her neighbourhood to pick up fruit and vegetable platters for a party that night. She failed to warn me said produce stand had not yet joined the 21st century and thus accepted only cash. They didn't even have a bank machine on the premises. Fortunately, it was one of those rare occasions I had some paper money in my billfold and was able to pay for the food and leave without incident. It was not always that way. It's only in the last ten or so years, with the digital revolution, that I do most of my transactions electronically with my banking card, even when ordering a pizza.

I traditionally have lunch with my father, brother and nephew at a buffet-style restaurant on New Year's Day. And every year my father picks up the tab by pulling a wad of cash from his right front trouser pocket and counting out the twenties until the bill is paid. It's always been like that with him. On top of that he does not have an actual wallet. The closest he has ever come is one of those simple, small, soft plastic fold-over pouches designed to hold your vehicle registration and insurance slips. His contains the aforementioned documents, as well as his driver's license, Social Insurance card, Canadian Citizenship Card, bank card and credit card. And he'd never carry this so-called wallet on him, instead choosing to leave it in his car's glove compartment, which despite the fact that his car has been robbed more times than a bad-neighbourhood 7-Eleven, he continues to feel it is the safest place on earth.

My father spent almost forty years as a cab driver back in the days when it was a cash on the barrelhead business, and the technology simply did not exist for taxis to accept credit cards. He owned his own car and permit, enjoying the independence the job gave him. If he needed more money, he could work extra hours. If he wanted to go on vacation, he wouldn't have to ask anyone's permission to have time off. He enjoyed the rare privilege of not having a real "Boss," just the once-in-a-while annoying customer and the taxi regulatory body. So when I was at Barclay Elementary and I broke one of my front teeth in the schoolyard, he was able to take me to the dentist in the middle of the day. All they had to do was call the cab company and he was there in less than two minutes. The taxi stand was on the same street as the school. He proudly has never been in debt or paid any interest; never carried a balance on a credit card, instead using it on the rare occasion when he did not have enough time to go to the bank, and only wrote cheques to pay things like the rent, and that was due to our Landlord's insistence.

I recall innumerable instances as a child when he'd buy something big, like furniture or a car. Upon completion of the deal, he'd pull out a huge bundle of bills from his brown polyester pants, and count out the amount needed. What would he do if he purchased something really expensive like a house? I'd imagine him with a humongoid wad, counting out twenties for hours.

After my parents divorced my mother would, on the first Saturday of the month, dispatch me to the taxi stand on the corner of Wiseman and Jarry to collect the alimony, which she referred to as what he owed for all the years she had wasted with him, and the child support. My father's pants were so loose and baggy that he could reach into his pocket and pull out the wad while still seated in his car. (Now that I think about it, it was probably deliberately done in order to easily access his cash and give his customers their change, as well as hide the amount he was carrying.) It was impossible to tell how much he had on him at any time, but somehow he always managed to have enough.

He'd carefully count out the scratch. "Here, this is for your mother," he'd dryly say with the first batch. "And this is for you and your brother," he'd say with the second.

Although notoriously tight-fisted, he would occasionally throw me an extra twenty and tell me to have a good time. I was never exactly sure what he meant, but I took the cash anyway, and did the best I could to enjoy myself. I never told him what I used if for, certain he wouldn't have approved of the activities that for me constituted "fun" like going to arcades or taking guitar lessons. Such things being, in his opinion, unnecessary, wasteful and distasteful.

By seventeen I had flunked out of high school and failed as a musician. Bored and listless, my father told me that if I went to college, he would pay for it entirely. Although I love learning, I never really enjoyed structured academic endeavours or thought myself the scholarly type (and that didn't include the social aspects of attending a public school, which presented to me an altogether different set of problems). I had the tendency of driving my teachers crazy with non-sequitur comments and what many of my classmates felt were oddball questions or observations. It was not uncommon for me to try to hijack the classroom and move the lesson more towards what I was interested in, and when we didn't I would totally zone out; some of my teachers liked me for that, but most did not appreciate what I did.

Almost all of my friends were already in CEGEP and I had no idea what else to do, so I gathered myself together and went to night school to finish my diploma and got into Dawson College, a place that back then did not have the entirely best reputation as an educational institute. At the beginning of every semester, like a living ATM, I would see him at the taxi stand where he would deal out the dough for tuition and books without complaint, and a few years later I had my DEC.

When I informed him that Concordia University had accepted my application, I could tell over the phone how happy he was, which was quite a big deal, considering this was the same man who, if I had called him while he was eating, would not put his meal on hold for two seconds to talk to me; instead I had to listen to loud, open-mouthed chewing noises while I spoke then struggled in vain to decipher his gruff, mumbled, full-mouth responses. As well he'd seldom say goodbye to me at the end of a phone communication, opting to simply grunt and hang up after deciding the conversation was over.

"Do you know what the proudest day of my life was?" he asked, after hearing I'd been accepted.

The day I was born? The day I became the first of his children to get into an accredited institution of higher education? One of my other achievements? Anything to do with me? Anything at all?

Of course not.

"It was the day *I* was accepted into college when I was a young man *een* Greece!" he said excitedly. My father had attended university for one year, but for reasons unexplained (at least to me anyway) he failed to complete his studies.

University was considerably more expensive than CEGEP, but Dad was still true to his word. I didn't have to go to Station 5, as the Wiseman and Jarry stand is known to the drivers of The Champlain Taxi Company, to collect the money for fees and books. This time he rushed right over to my apartment in Snowdon to deliver the *dinero*, as well as a box of celebratory doughnuts. (I'm still uncertain why he did *that* … I was never really into doughnuts; was it some sort of family tradition or something?) And of course out came the wad with exactly the amount required, and he reliably continued to do so until I graduated, not once asking to see a bill or receipt.

I never had the heart to tell him I deposited the money in my bank account, paid the tuition with a cheque, and put the books on my credit card. I imagine he'd harrumph his disappointment.

THE MONOPOLY

Growing up I never dared to imagine that one day I'd wear a communication device on my belt that would enable me to make calls whenever I wanted, just like Captain Kirk; not to mention miracles of science like caller I.D., text messaging, camera phones, voice mail, call waiting, smart phones, or MP3 players.

My favourite telephone tale began one night when I was about four years old. My father shouted: "Dina! *Ellah etho!*" ['Come here!'] excitedly as he entered our Birnam Street flat, carrying some sort of contraband in a wrinkled old brown paper bag.

"*Ellah na thees efto!*" ['Come see this!'] he said.

We all rushed into the kitchen, where Dad emptied contents of the large bag onto the dinner table.

"Oh my!" my mother said, gasping. "*Pou toh vrikes efto?*" ['Where did you find that?']

"Someone at the taxi stand sold *eet* to me!" he declared.

Station 5 was notorious in Park Extension as a magnet for every low-life sleezoid petty thief and scuzzo loser hocking ill-gotten loot. Dad once had his taxi radio stolen, only to buy it back later that same day from the very thief who ripped it off, so I guess his radio was more kidnapped than stolen. Especially prolific in the hot merchandise department was a long-haired and seedy-looking man who roamed Park Ex in a beat-up faded blue late model Chevy we all called "The Guy in the Blue Van." More than once he'd call me over as I walked down the street as a teenager and offer to sell me stereo speakers or a 10-speed bike. I was always cautious not to get too close to him and turn him down politely with a "no, thank you" and "have a good day" just to be sure not to get on his bad side. I mean, who knew what else was in the back of that van?

My brother and I were anxious to see what all the excitement was about. When we finally squeezed our way past Mom and Dad, we were shocked to discover what was on the table: A telephone. A stout, flat black, rotary dial telephone with a cord that looked like it was violently yanked from its jack.

Today the telephone is a piece of technology that all Western society takes for granted. When I was a child, however, the Telephone Company was a monopoly. Only they were permitted by law to provide telecommunication services. And if you wanted a phone, you had no choice but to rent it from them. Telephone ownership for private citizens was out of the question.

There was no such thing as a cordless phone, and the unit's wire could not be removed from the jacks, so its roving radius was limited to about ten feet, unless one leased a phone with one of those ridiculously long cords that could stretch from here to China and often entangled small children and large sea mammals if they weren't careful.

The luxury and expense of two telephones in the same household could only be afforded by the C.E.O.'s of multi-national corporations, the President of the United States of America, the Emperor of Japan, and The Pope. Telephones were especially a status symbol for my mother, who grew up poor in the mountains of Greece. Her hometown was barely a town at all, but more like a loose association of a dozen or so houses and a church, all built into the side of a mountain and divided in two by a winding, at the time unpaved road.

About a year before she left there as a teenager, someone in the town got a telephone. Everyone from miles around rode their donkeys over to see the marvellous, magical device. He even started a little business, charging people to use the phone. He would have made money too, if the only people in the village knew someone else with a phone to call.

In order to defend their monopoly, the Telephone Company would from time to time put inserts into the bills they mailed out that read like Orwellian propaganda. I recall one that announced that there would soon be two varieties of telephones available in three flat, bland colours. Order now and you may receive one of these fine new units in three to five years!*

Supply is limited. All orders subject to government approval on a case by case basis. The Telephone Company reserves the right to refuse service to anyone, even for not liking their face. What are you going to do about it? We're a MONOPOLY, loser! You have a problem with that? Didn't think so!

Mom and Dad swore us to secrecy, and warned that our family would be in serious jeopardy if it were discovered that we had an illegal telephone. My parents, one must understand, grew up under Nazi occupation, as well as several other not-so-free regimes, and had an instinctive fear and distrust of any authority. To this day, even though she has had citizenship for over fifty-five years, my mother still fears sudden deportation.

They spun for us a tale of armed men kicking down our door and storming our house like some sort of Telephone Company Gestapo. They would then separate us; my parents would be sent back to Greece, and my brother would be sentenced to some Dickensian children's forced labour facility where we would make leather Oxford shoes for the offspring of Telephone Company executives. I, on the other hand, was young enough to be sent to a Telephone Company re-education camp where I would be brainwashed into loving huge monopoly corporations, and later work as one of those creepy drones who install the phone lines in people's houses.

My parents told us that, if anyone were to ask, the phone was already in the house when we moved in. Dad then scraped the "Property of The One and Only Telephone Company … DO NOT remove under penalty of deportation" sticker off the bottom. If caught, he probably figured he'd pretend not to be able to speak English or French, and use the old ignorant immigrant excuse that occasionally got him out of traffic tickets.

The items my father brought home that "fell off a truck" were more often than not in poor condition, rarely worked properly and usually found their way to the garbage a week later. The new telephone, however, was no lemon; we used it for several years without any problems.

My father decided to install it into the unused jack in my parents' bedroom. Tampering with the phone lines was strictly verboten, but the way he saw it he had already gone this far, so why not go all the way? Besides, Dad thought that calling someone who knew how to install a black market telephone would just create another witness he would have to eliminate.

Dad grew up on a farm and was very handy around the house, albeit sometimes clumsy. My mother would often remark that in order to repair something, Dad had to break something else. So if he were to fix a chair, he would damage the ironing board. Fixing the ironing board somehow damaged the frying pan. Fixing the frying pan broke the coffee table, and so on. Dad was always working on one damn thing after another, in a perpetual loop of Sisyphean frustration.

A political activist in Greece, Dad was more adept at making Molotov cocktails, pipe bombs, and various other items of political expression from regular household items. But repairing complex electronic and mechanical items at times brought him nothing but sorrow.

When we rented the house on L'Acadie Boulevard, in the garage the last tenants left an old lawnmower. My father spent most of our first summer there trying to get the damn thing to work. He would take the engine apart, reassemble it, and then angrily yank on the starter cord for hours to no avail. He never got it close to starting. Not even the tease of a brief sputter. Eventually the grass grew so high my brother and I couldn't play in the yard without machetes, so my mother decided to call the landlord and asked him to have it done. Two guys with huge mowers came by and cut the front and back yards in less than twenty minutes.

It took several tries, but my father finally got the telephone working properly, and we were suddenly elevated one notch on the old social ladder above most everyone else in Park Ex. But of course, we couldn't tell anyone, lest they jealously snitch on us to score some points with the phone company.

I remember my brother and I played with the phones. We were too young to have anyone to call, but if we each picked up one of the receivers, we could talk to each other from different rooms the way other children would play with two cans and a string. It was even better than having a walkie-talkie, because we used devices perceived as being exclusively for grown-ups.

A few years later the phone company relaxed its iron grip, allowed for removable phone jacks, and opened a chain of ridiculous telephone boutiques designed to appease the proletariat with the illusion of choice. My father had converted the ill-gotten device to one with a removable plug, (after a few unsuccessful tries) and we were again set.

The phone stores were a joke. The service was poor, and not a single outlet was in a convenient location. The closest one to where we lived was in a building above the Jean-Talon metro station called *Tour Jean-Talon*, (which translates to Jean Talon Tower ... odd considering it *towered* to about 10 storeys and was more of a huge glass and cement block than what someone with any sophistication would refer to as a *tower*), at the time a brief ride on the Number 92 bus away.

What's more, now that they had retail outlets, the lineman who installed the phones no longer delivered the product you wanted to your door, or serviced the telephones themselves. Whereas before if your phone didn't work, the phone company would send someone to replace it (you'd have to, of course, take a sabbatical from work to wait for them), now there was no option. It wasn't like you could go to the store at a convenient time, or have them deliver the phone. Now you had to go to the phone store, and wait in a Soviet-like breadline. And the stores were only open Monday to Friday, from 10 a.m. to 5 p.m. A person had to either leave work early or arrive late in order to get a sarcasm laden encounter with a telephone boutique employee.

The line-ups were more depressing than a puppy's funeral. Women were known to smother their crying babies for fear of losing their place.

Once my brother and I spent a professional day off from school in one of the boutiques trying to exchange a defective phone. The clerk slipped away quickly as she was serving us, returning soon after with an evil grin on her face. She pushed a button behind her counter that summoned a uniformed guard in jackboots and automatically shut the doors.

"I called your home number. Someone there answered. According to our records, you only have one phone from us, and it's the one you just turned in! What's going on? Do you have two phones? A black rotary telephone was stolen in your neighbourhood several years ago? Do you know anything about this?"

I thought the jig was up, and was about to panic and spill my guts in exchange for preferential sentencing in phone court. Fortunately, my tacit and deceptively keen brother stepped in to save the day.

"One of our neighbours lent us one of his phones because our mother was expecting an important call today."

"Oh," the clerk said, with a look on her face that was more like: *Okay … you win this round!* She called off her goons and allowed us to eventually leave the premises.

The phone company once tried to soften its image as a cold, heartless, faceless monopoly by selling limited edition children's toys at the phone stores. The "toys" were plush, shaped like a standard rotary phone, and had an eerie set of smiling cardboard lips glued to the front. They knew that kids were tired of cuddling stuffed renditions of warm and fuzzy creatures like bear cubs as they slept, and were now ready to embrace a piece of technology. They would soon enough be correct … sort of.

Eventually the government relaxed their restrictive laws and allowed for the free market competition that brought us the cordless and cellular communication technological revolutions for which the masses had longed. The same legislation probably disbanded the phone cops and shut down the re-education camps and forced labour factories.

Viva la revolución!

THE TIME I DID NOT MEET
PIERRE ELLIOTT TRUDEAU

My current job has a few perks, one of which is I get to meet and hob-nob with quite a few famous people. I enjoy getting photographs with them and posting said shots on various social media platforms in the hopes of attaining the "likes" which sustain me. I do it so often in fact that more than once my friends have enquired as to whether or not I had a room or photo album full of such pictures. (And I do…a digital one, that is!) But it was not always the case with me. I once had a habit of missing really cool opportunities.

When I was at university one of my instructors, a graduate student not much older than his students, would hold end-of-semester parties at his place, a large second-floor flat on Clark Street he shared with his roommate, another grad student. At one such soiree the roommate went around asking everyone if they wanted to go to a bar the next night and see a hot new act. I asked what the band was called, and when he told me the name, I laughed in his face and turned him down. Ultimately there were only a dozen or so people at the gig in question, and the audience got to hang and party with the band afterwards. The group: Smashing Pumpkins.

A few years later I was working at a record store and my manager asked if I wanted two tickets to an album launch party in Old Montreal that night. When I asked who the act was, he said it was a new release by someone from Ottawa who was once on a silly children's comedy show CJOH television produced that I didn't care for. He even showed me her first effort, a CD of dance tunes made when she was still a teenager.

"Thanks but no thanks," I said. So he gave the tickets to his friend.

Once again there were only a handful of people at that show, and they audience got to hang out with the singer. Who was she? Alanis Morissette. And the album was the '90's mega-monster *Jagged Little Pill*.

But the story of how I did not meet The Right Honourable Pierre Elliott Trudeau, the Prime Minister of Canada? That was my first and to this day greatest missed opportunity.

It happened when I was still a student at Barclay Elementary. Barclay was a rather large educational institution, with five or six different classes per grade, and often a teacher had over thirty pupils per classroom. Students shuffled from year to year; sometimes they would move away to New Bordeaux or Chomedey. New students were always coming in, so one rarely had the same classmates two years in a row. Because we spent all day together, it was not uncommon to change best friends on an annual basis.

Being terminally uncool and always odd man out, even by elementary school standards, I was a hard luck case when it came to making quality friends. Because I did not talk with a Greek accent and didn't use Greek words, colloquialisms, terms and curses, I was often shunned as an outsider. More than once I was asked by other students if I was Greek at all, as if my name and face didn't give it away. I never understood why that was so important to them.

In Grade 5 I lucked out with a kid named Mike P. He was a diminutive skateboarder that later reminded me of Marty McFly from *Back to the Future*. Mike P. would follow around the cool kids in the schoolyard trying to break into the group, but because of his size they just bullied him, so he ended up with me as a consolation prize. We got along well, and with another kid named Dennis, we had a decent clique.

Because Dennis was a latchkey kid who had to take his younger brother home after school and look out for him until his parents returned from work, it was mostly myself and Mike P. who hung out or went late afternoon bike riding. But he was never available on Fridays. When I asked him why he told me it was because he had his scout meetings.

"You're in the Boy Scouts?" I asked. We had only been friends for a few weeks, so I had no clue about this. I was unaware that there was a chapter in Park Ex, let alone one exclusively for kids from the Greek community.

He described to me how much fun it was, and said I should join.

"It would give us a chance to hang out together more often," he said.

There are three Greek Orthodox churches on St. Roch Avenue (I couldn't be bothered to learn their actual names): The one on the corner of Wiseman that burned down in the '70's (rebuilt decades later; in the interim, the dedicated priest, so pious he felt that bathing was a sin and could be smelled two churches over, continued to hold services in the burned-out building's basement until the city ordered him to stop for safety reasons, forcing him to hold Sunday mass on street corners), the big blue one with the massively tall steeple (which caught fire a few times, but never burnt down completely … so far), and a little further east is the small brown one (eventually it burned down as well, and was subsequently rebuilt). Our scout troop met in the basement of the small brown one. The next Friday Mike P. brought me to the meeting. There were several boys there I knew from school, or around the neighbourhood, and even a few friends of Peter's. There were also two brothers my family used to know, Jimmy K. and his younger brother Laki, whose mother was a widow my parents befriended. We used to take them for beach outings, picnics, barbeques, and the like years before. I had not seen those guys for some time and they were teenagers now, but they remembered me. The rest of the boys there were of various ages and I didn't know any of them. I felt relatively comfortable there already acquainted with a few of them, and I was welcomed warmly by the scout leader, a short, lean twentysomething who was in great shape and dressed in a tight white t-shirt and jeans, much like The Fonz (probably deliberately so, as *Happy Days* was a hit show at the time), named Chris M. His younger brother George M., a portly, plodding slacker, was also one of the scouts in our troop.

The next day my mother took me to the downtown Simpson's store, where one could purchase a Boy Scouts of Canada uniform at the time. Mom watched with pride as the sales lady showed me how to wear my beret and sash properly. I was set and eager to make new friends.

It was during my second meeting that Chris M. had some business to attend to in the small office he used in the church basement, and left one of the older boys in charge of going through drills with us. The moment they are given any type of authority, most Greeks will abuse said powers before exhaling. The new man in temporary charge was a wispy-moustached teenager, considerably taller than I was, and was not an exception to that rule. I'm not sure why, but he zeroed in on me right away. He said I wasn't standing at attention properly and angrily berated me for that, his face mere inches from mine. Then he roughly man-handled me as he adjusted my stance, called me a spaz, and as *la pièce de résistance*, he slapped me across the face. I immediately slapped him back. A resounding chorus of "Ooooh-hhhs" came from the other scouts and the drillmaster stood there shocked, embarrassed, and then irate. He shoved me to the ground and kicked me once on the leg. When the others saw how serious he was they intervened. When Chris M. came back in, none of us told him what happened. I was tempted to but didn't, certain he would have been unsympathetic.

Everything went well for a couple of weeks, then disaster struck: Mike P.'s father bought a small local grocery store on Bernard Street which he named *Le Petit Marché Parfait*. He expected Mike P. to work there after school and on weekends, stocking shelves and making deliveries on one of those ubiquitous three-wheeled bicycles, so he could no longer attend the meetings or other activities.

I didn't want to quit because my Mom had spent something like $60 for the uniform, and as a child I had a problem sticking with commitments. I was always taking up a hobby or activity, and then giving up when it became too difficult, or I started to lose interest. I promised myself I would stay with this, and I did … for a while. I gave it my best shot. By Christmas I had earned a half dozen merit badges and my attendance was perfect.

At a subsequent meeting Chris M. lost it with his brother's insubordination and laziness, so he brought out a big punishment: a heavy plastic bucket filled with I don't know what but when someone other than Chris M. handled it they could barely get it off the ground, much less control the monster. He made George M. hold it out in front of him with his arms stretched out, a task worthy of Hercules. A few weeks later Chris M. caught his brother sneaking into his room at home trying to find copies of the upcoming neckerchief exam we had to do about the life of Baden-Powell. George M.'s punishment, besides being called-out and humiliated in front of all of us to a degree that made me very uncomfortable, was to get on the floor in a mid-push-up position as Chris M. sat on the floor at an angle with his feet just below his brother's crotch. As George M. struggled to stay up, his brother gave him a dressing down, calling him a "fat pig."

I started to dread the thought of ever getting on Chris M.'s bad side. During marching practice one evening he stopped the procession, pulled me out and let me have it verbally for the way I swung my arms "like a retard," aping my arm movements in front of the others. I was so scared I stood there speechless, fearful he was about to give me some physically difficult punishment. But he didn't, and we continued marching.

One Saturday the troop went to see a movie together. It was called *Hardly Working* starring fading screen actor Jerry Lewis, and was playing at the Van Horne cinema on the corner of Van Horne and Côte-des-Neiges, which was right across from a McDonald's. We were waiting in line for admission, and I had a few extra dollars, so I asked Chris M. if I could quickly run over and get some fries. When he said okay, Laki and two other boys joined me. I got my small fries and a soda and returned right away to the line at the theatre. Laki and the other boys decided to stay there for a bit. When they eventually got back, Chris M. was furious.

"Where were you fucking assholes?" he said.

"What?" Laki asked. "What do you mean?"

"You were supposed to come back right away!"

"I didn't know ..."

"Look! This guy, here," Chris M. said, pointing at me, "he came right back!"

"What's the big deal?" Laki asked. With that Chris M. grabbed Laki's shake from his hands and crushed it right before his eyes, and then spiked it like a football.

"There! Happy now?" Chris M. said.

"Hey!" Laki protested

"*What's the big deal?*" Chris M. replied sarcastically.

When we got inside Chris M. had cooled down and with a hint of remorse offered to buy Laki something from the candy counter.

"No, it's okay," Laki said, looking despondent.

I had finally had enough around Easter time. We had a big get together with other scout troops, including the Cub Scouts, Ventures, and the Girl Scouts, in the cavernous basement of the big blue church. We had competitive activities and did some skits. I, always the clumsy and awkward one, did not excel in any of the competitive games, which cost our troop some ribbons. Some of the guys let me have it worse than when Charlie Brown brought back the lame tree in the *Peanuts Christmas Special*; no one consoled or stood up for me either. I lurched home feeling alienated. After all those months of trying, I could not make one new friend among my troop.

Not long after it was late spring and the weather was beautiful, so we were going to have a co-ed softball game with the Girl Guides. I was not a great athlete to begin with, and had never played an organized game of softball before. I borrowed my brother's bat and glove, and left for the game. When I rounded St. Roch and headed towards the church, I started getting a queasy feeling in the pit of my stomach. I imagined myself striking out, or failing to make a catch, or otherwise screwing up, and everyone there ganging up on me and laughing. In front of the girls on top of than. I stopped dead in my tracks. I just couldn't do it. So I turned around and went home. And for the first time ever I missed a meeting.

"Why back so soon?" Mom asked me.

"I'm ... I'm not feeling well," I said.

I never went back. No one in my family ever asked me why. They just figured I disappointed them again by giving up on yet another good thing.

A few weeks later one of the kids from our troop, and older boy named Perry who lived across from us on Stuart, stopped me on the street and asked if I planned to return to the scouts.

"Nope," I said. I was so embarrassed and a little ashamed for being a quitter that I didn't even bother to make eye contact with him and abruptly walked away. I'm not sure why I was so rude to Perry; he was one of the better guys and never gave me any grief.

The following September my brother and I were watching the local six o'clock news. They were doing an "in other news" segment, which was usually a quick series of video clips with a voiceover from Bill Haugland, the local news anchor, briefly explaining what was happening.

"A group of local boy scouts met the Prime Minister today," he said. "The scouts were from Montreal's Greek community ..."

And the image they used on the screen? Mike P. smiling like an idiot and shaking hands with Pierre Trudeau.

When the hell did Mike P. start going back to the meetings?

"Hey, isn't that you friend? Just think, if you didn't quit the scouts, you'd have met Trudeau and been on the news right now!" Peter said.

Thanks for your insight and analysis! It was most enlightening!

During his tenure as Prime Minister Pierre Trudeau was the most famous Canadian in the world. The first time I went to Greece in 1977 everyone I met asked where I was from. When I told them to a person they said: *"Kanadas? Nai, oh Pierre Trudeau!"* as they nodded and smiled broadly.

I remember watching the news the day Pierre Trudeau died. They were asking people on the street for their reaction. A teenaged girl said she saw him almost every day as he walked to work and wanted to approach him just to say "Hi" and she now regretted never having the courage to do that, forever losing her opportunity.

At least I'm not the only one.

THE LEGEND OF SHITBOY MONSTER

When I was about seven my family lived on the top floor of a duplex on Stuart Avenue. Our landlord was a kindly old man named Mr. Davitz. Next to the house was a parking space for my Dad's car. Because Mr. Davitz was so old, and all of his grandchildren were grown, my brother and I had the backyard pretty much to ourselves, and beyond its fence was a narrow grassy strip owned by the city. It divided the block in half, and served as a playground for the children who lived one street over on Wiseman Avenue, whose properties didn't have the good fortune of containing room for backyards or gardens.

Peter and I arrived in the lane one summer morning to find a whole gang of kids assembled in a circle, using sticks to poke and prod what looked like a pile of sand. Upon closer examination it turned out to be a huge pile of used kitty litter dumped by some asshole damn smack in the middle of our playground. The mystery of who did it and why was never solved.

Using their sticks, several of the children tried to gross everyone out by attempting to flick some of the deposits in the pile on others, but they only succeeded in hitting some of the gang with a few gross grains of the litter. Then one of the younger ones, a skinny, pale boy with a hook nose and elephant ears, saw an opportunity to distinguish himself in the history of Park Ex and gathered enough nerve to pick up one of the larger pieces of shit with his bare hand, using it to threaten the other kids. They scattered like scared rabbits in all directions, with the young boy hot in pursuit, excrement clasped firmly in his hand.

An adult in one of the surrounding houses finally noticed this from her back balcony and eventually came down with a shovel and garbage bag and cleaned up the mess. But the damage had already been done. The boy, whose real name I didn't know, began to refer to himself as "Shitboy Monster." For some incomprehensible reason, this became to him some sort of misguided badge of honour; perhaps being known as Shitboy Monster was better than dwelling in anonymity? Until that day, most of the other kids never gave him a second thought. Now he had a nickname. Now he was unique.

As time went by, Shitboy and his family moved away. Mr. Davitz died and the new landlord evicted us by saying that his oldest son was about to get married and they needed the place for him and his new wife, whom they were importing for Portugal. Quebec law allows for this common landlord dodge as a technicality that is abused by owners who want to evict a tenant even if they always paid the rent on time, like we did. We were there for so long and Mr. Davitz had not raised the monthly rate for years, so our place was a real bargain. After we left the marriage was conveniently called off. They could not hide that from us because we moved right next door to a brand new slim triplex built where our former parking space was. I wanted to sue, but Mom preferred to just let it go. My family soon scattered like little children being chased by some idiot kid waving around a piece of shit.

Years later, my mother insisted I see a newsletter from her church. She made it a point to show me a photo of a half dozen newly ordained Greek Orthodox priests who were from the Montreal area.

"So what?" I said. "I really don't care about that sort of thing. You know that."

"*Ré*, stupid guy! I said look at the *facking* picture, *axristos!*" [Loosely translates as 'good for nothing.'] Mom said in her usual polite, respectful, pleasant, and diplomatic way.

Upon second glance, I was flabbergasted.

"Hey! Is that ... no ... it can't be!"

"*Nai*," Mom said, "*enai o* Shitboy! *Eftos exi yini Pappas! Kai esi? Ti kanis mais to zoë sou?*" ['Yes, it's Shitboy! He has become a Priest! And you? What are you doing with your life?']

She had me there. Shitboy had done pretty well for himself. And what was I doing with my life? Working at a record store. Not married. Not even a girlfriend at the time. Never thought a guy who once referred to himself as "Shitboy Monster," and proudly so, would end up anywhere other than a circus sideshow. I especially would not have envisioned him as a holy man.

I wonder how those who attend his services would feel about taking communion from someone who, as a boy, had no qualms about not only touching, but closing his hand on rotting cat feces, and gave himself the moniker Shitboy Monster? And do they call him Father Shitboy now?

"Is he going to be the priest at one of the St. Roch churches?" I asked. "Or another one in Park Ex?"

"No," Mom said, "he *eez* going to *Another Stage*."

"*Another Stage*" is what my mother calls the United States. And it's not a simple misunderstanding of her thick Greek accent. She literally says "*Another Stage*." Whenever I tried to explain to her that it's actually *United States* she would say: "No! There *eez* one stage, and then there *eez* Another Stage. Europe *waz* the first stage, *kai teen Ameriquis enai Another Stage*."

That was not her only personal alteration to the English language. When Mom wanted to call someone an idiot, she would say "*in-dee-an*" as in "he *eez* a stupid *in-dee-an*!" I tried to correct her, but she insisted it was "*in-dee-an*" and not idiot. To date I have not asked her if she thought the word was "indian" or if she was simply mispronouncing it, which does happen, or if she believed it to be a mysterious third word, out of fear of what her answer may be.

Another term Mom would employ for those lacking in the brain department was "*nee-coal head*," her version of knucklehead. In my ongoing and continually disappointing quest to explain her errors I said that it was in fact "knucklehead." When she asked what a knuckle was I showed her by pointing at my hand. She laughed at me as though I were the ridiculous one.

"So, explain the expression to me then," I said.

"You see, someone who *eez* stupid, their head *eez* worth five cent. So they are *nee-coal head, katalavenis?*" ['Do you understand?']

How could I argue with that?

My favourite term Mom invented was "*under-the-neath*" instead of saying underneath. If something was on top, it somehow for her wasn't "*over-the-neath*." And what exactly is a "*neath*" anyways? When I asked her elaborate she refused to answer.

If my mom spoke of a food item she enjoyed, she would say "*eet eez thee-licious*." So it is so wonderful it goes beyond just plain old "*licious*" no, it is the definition, the epitome of "*licious*." Silly me I tried to correct her by saying it was in reality "*de*-licious" and Mom would say that the "de" prefix implied it was in fact *anti-licious*, the very opposite of her "*thee-licious*."

Once again I found that logic difficult to debate.

I had a customer when I was working years later who was a middle-aged Greek woman. She came up to my wicket and said: "I *djust* have a *tseck*."

"*Djust* a *tseck*? And what are you having for dinner tonight? *Tsi-ken*?"

The customer shot me a serious glare and asked in Greek if I made fun of my mother like that.

"Yes. Yes I do," I answered with a smile, fully aware that my evil, disrespectful ways would eventually land me in Hell.

I find it amusing how Shitboy ... oh sorry, *Father* Shitboy got his nickname by handling excrement, and now he makes a living by shovelling it.

I also find it a little inspirational that in this world, even a creepy, skinny, goofy kid branded *Shitboy Monster* could rebound and become a spiritual leader for an entire congregation. It just goes to show that in life, no one has a clue what's going to happen. And there's hope for all the Shitboys out there.

Unless you are a "*nee-coal headed*" "*in-dee-an*" from "*Another Stage*."

THE MUSIC MAN

Of my twenty-plus first cousins, I am the youngest male. When I was school-aged I spent most holidays and weekends with my extended family, primarily those on my mother's side, and was greatly influenced by two older cousins who were into Heavy Metal. I didn't really pay much attention to music in elementary school mostly because I was deeply into *Star Wars*, but once I got to Outremont High the last film was released and I needed something new to obsess over, so I began to take an interest, like the world was at the time, in hard rock. But I had one problem: my father. He was strict, old-fashioned, did not understand my generation (there is an almost forty-year age different between us) and would never allow me to grow my hair long and wear three-quarter length sleeve baseball shirts depicting images of Eddie from Iron Maiden or Ozzy Osbourne. In fact, not only did he select my high school, he chose a program that didn't leave any room for the arts, which I would have preferred. No, he had a different plan for my brother and me, exemplified by a car trip to *Université de Montréal* on a Sunday afternoon when we were children.

"Here," he proudly declared, "*eez* where you two will go to university!"

"But I was thinking of going to McGill," my brother said. I said nothing because I was eight at the time and had no ambitions in life beyond getting my hands on more *Star Wars* action figures.

"Ahh!" Dad said, as he waved his hand in a dismissing motion. "McGill *eez* full of *Anglaisis*! If you go here you will learn French, and then you can work for the government! You have to know French to work for the government!"

Dad always believed that the highest achievement a human can aspire to was to be some kind of bureaucrat or civil servant, and he could not understand our lack of enthusiasm for such a career choice. Even back then I knew for sure that I didn't want to pursue such a vocation.

But luck was on my side. After I finished my disastrous 7th grade, my parents divorced. And I was free. Despite having full custody Mom still let Dad be in charge of our education, but at least now I was free to be me at home if not at school.

Iron Maiden was touring Canada that summer in support of their new album *Piece of Mind* (a tour they cleverly called the World *Piece* Tour) and my brother, two of our cousins, and I, pooled our cash and waited by the radio each morning for the concert announcement. We were at the Forum twenty minutes after the radio declared Iron Maiden was coming in September and scored 14th row orchestra seats. Dad would never had allowed us to do that, let alone actually attend the concert.

The show was amazing, and the next day I strutted around school in my official souvenir tour shirt and huge afro that I grew over the summer. One of my teachers laughed when she saw me and how had I uncharacteristically changed from a total geek to a rocker (although admittedly still quite geeky). And I knew what I wanted to do: Be a rock star.

I asked my father for a guitar for Christmas. (In those days there were two schools of rock, both ruled by men born with the name "James." One either was a disciple of Jimmy Page of Led Zeppelin and wanted a low-slung cherry-starburst Gibson Les Paul guitar or they were a devotee of Jimi Hendrix and desired a Strat. I was the latter.)

I brought my father a fan magazine with an ad for Fender that had the exact axe I wanted: a yellow and black Fender Stratocaster.

"Okay," he strangely agreed, but continued with a dire warning, "but don't think you will ever be professional."

It wasn't until my fourteenth birthday that I finally got my instrument. A music store on Sherbrooke near Decarie was having a sale and I nagged my father into finally keeping his word and buying what I had long desired. The fact that it would be on sale was the clincher. So we went on a sunny Saturday afternoon. His friend *Archidias* tagged along for some reason. When we arrived the best gear was still too expensive, so we compromised and got an imitation Strat from a company called Profile with a maple neck and fingerboard, but it looked and sounded like a real Strat. The instrument in question did not have a metal rod inserted in the neck, the way real Strats do, to prevent it from bending, as the Profile did a year later, making it difficult to keep in tune.

I sat in the back seat of my Dad's Chevy as we drove back home. *Archidias* leaned over to my dad and, likely thinking that I did not understand Greek, said to him: "Do you really think your kid is going to learn to play? You just wasted your money. He's a loser."

Dad just grunted. I don't know if he agreed, or just didn't like the fact that he spent some money. But I didn't care. I had what I wanted.

I began to bang away day and night ... to no avail. I had ordered lessons from an ad in the back of a fan magazine, but they were no help. I knew I would have to take lessons from an actual person; a live teacher to answer questions and correct my mistakes if I were to ever improve.

Another aspiring rock star I knew from school was able to connect me with a musician who was once a member of a successful mid-level '70's hard rock band and now gave lessons on the side. The sessions were $20 each (affordable) and irregular so I could have them whenever I had the cash available.

I was so excited when I booked my first lesson that I showed up an hour early to his Shaughnessy Village apartment. I was going to see how a genuine real-life rock star lived! What I found was a messy, dusty one-room apartment, its walls lined with fading mementos, occupied by a male hippie rocker version of Gloria Swanson from *Sunset Boulevard* who was always so broke that he would empty out cigarette butts from his overflowing ashtray and squeeze out that last little bit of unused tobacco onto a piece of rolling paper to form one final, desperate smoke before having to go and buy another pack of du Maurier regulars. But still, I thought it was cool. Before the initial lesson I went to Sam the Record Man and checked out some old releases from his band. It was the first time I met in person someone whom I had seen on a record album.

Before we began the lesson he took out some weed and a tiny, palm-sized bong and lit up. Growing up in Park Ex illicit drug use was rampant, but most people used out of sight in back alleys or under balconies and all we'd see are glimpses here and there of older teenagers toking weed or junkies shooting up, and everything in between. I had never seen anyone do something like that in front of me so openly before. Once the lesson started I could see he knew what he was doing and eventually I was taking lessons from him two or three times a month.

I developed a routine: Every Saturday I would go downtown and, starting from the Atwater Metro, walk up Ste. Catherine Street perusing record stores, looking for interesting new groups and trying (unsuccessfully) to meet girls. My personal favourite place was the now defunct Rock En Stock, located on Crescent Street. They had the coolest new metal imports from Europe. I would then work my way to Steve's Music on St. Antoine and buy a new set of strings, and go home to restring my axe with a fresh, lively set. Lessons were mostly on Sundays, whenever The Music Man was not out of town on a gig with one of several bands he played with at the time, or at a recording session. Other days I would practice sixty to ninety minutes, sometimes two hours a day.

And I slowly started to get better.

One afternoon I showed up at The Music Man's place, and he seemed a little anxious.

"Can I have the $20 in advance today?" he asked.

"Sure," I said.

When I took it out of my pocket and held it up, without hesitation he snatched it out of my hand like a cat batting at a ball on the end of a string.

"Thanks, that's really cool of you," he said as he started to leave. "Get set up I'll be right back."

He returned a few minutes later with a bag of weed and immediately lit up his bong. I stared at him as he inhaled as deeply as he could and said, jokingly: "Gee, is my playing that bad?"

He momentarily looked up at me with an angry eye as if to say "fuck you, punk!"

The sessions continued for years; if I had taken them more often I might have become a slightly better player. But what I enjoyed were the few minutes before and after when he would regale me with tales of drug- and alcohol-fuelled mayhem on the road and banging groupies two at a time. He also told me stories of how he was screwed out of royalties and had a team of lawyers trying to get his money from the States. I was suspicious of how someone living in a one-room Shaughnessy Village apartment and who dug through ashtrays for cigarette butts could possibly afford to have one lawyer, let alone a "team" to hunt down a few pennies on the dollar. But what did I know?

There were more concerts, more lessons, and I practiced as much as I could. I became so obsessed with rock and roll that I often could not think or talk about anything else. Once my art teacher threw a monster fit and cursed me out in Arabic when she saw me draw for the millionth time a rocker with a guitar in front of a Japanese rising sun for a project. No matter what we were working in art class, I found a way to incorporate an image like that.

I had begun to write songs and kept them all in a notebook I carried around with me just about everywhere. One of the songs, called "Cold Wind Blowing" had a chorus that went like this:

> *I can feel the cold wind blowing*
> *Taking me away from you*
> *Don't know where I'm going*
> *Don't know what to do*

One could see the last line coming up St. Laurent Street. It was the greatest lyrics since KISS brilliantly rhymed "baby" with "baby" and "me" with "me."

The chorus of another song, called "Makin' My Way" went like this:

> *'Cause I'm walking (talkin')*
> *movin' (groovin')*
> *cruisin' (loosin')*
> *makin' my way*
> *Yes I'm walking (talkin')*
> *movin' (groovin')*
> *cruisin' (loosin')*
> *makin' my way*
> *makin' my way*
> *makin' my way*
> (guitar solo)

Even Aerosmith fans would find those lyrics derivative, tired and trite.

I used to bring fan magazines to the lesson that I bought at a Multi-mags located one street over from The Music Man's place. Whenever I did he would ridicule me and say things like: "That's not a serious musician's magazine! That's a cheap rag that tells you who Joe Elliot is fucking!" When I pointed out to him the columns with pro tips on how to improve one's playing in the last few pages of said publications, he became even more irate.

"That's just bullshit stuff for amateurs and wanna-be's! If those musicians were any good technically, they would be writing for serious music journals like *Guitar World* or *Guitar Player*, not some shitty fan mag! I bet they didn't even write the pieces themselves. They're probably done by some record company's promotional department!"

He then grabbed a copy of *Guitar World* magazine from a pile he had in his living room/bedroom/parlour/salon/kitchen/dining room and waved it in my face saying "this! This is a real musician's magazine! Start buying these and stop wasting your time reading that worthless crap."

Ultimately he was right. And how good could the journalism have been in those fan mags, anyway? With all their investigating somehow the hard-nosed news hounds at *Hit Parader* and *Circus* completely missed that Rob Halford and Freddie Mercury were gay.

So I immediately went back to Multimags and bought the latest issues of *Guitar World* and *Guitar Player*.

But those publications were way too dry and technical. *Guitar Player* was okay because it had sheet music to rock songs with chord charts and the tablature underneath so I was able to pick up a few songs and it helped me when I started to learn how to read sheet music. But *Guitar World* was way over my head. It was an experienced, professional musician's publication. It failed to hold my interest. (I guess I did really care more about who Joe Elliot was fucking.)

When I was baffled by something in a *Guitar World* article I would telephone The Music Man and ask him if he could clarify. At first he was cooperative and helpful, but when I started calling too often (and several times more than once a day) with questions, he began getting sore at me and said I should save my inquiries for the next lesson, adding in exasperation: "I don't live solely to help you, y'know!" I think he just didn't want to give out free advice. So I thought: *To hell with him! I'm going to audition for Vanier's music program, and when I get in, I won't have to take any more lesson from that guy!*

I eventually tried out for a couple of bands, but I never made the cut. One summer I took a theory and ear training course at the McGill Conservatory of Music to prepare for the aforementioned audition at Vanier. But there was one more thing to do: Prove to the whole student body that I was a bona-fide potential rock star at The Outremont High School Spring Talent Show.

I bought new clothes and practiced my routine: an Eddie Van Halen-like guitar solo that lasted about five minutes. I prepared both musically and my moves in front of the hall mirror until I thought I had the bit down solid.

The audition was after school and I brought my new blood-red Kramer K-1000 guitar (endorsed by none other than Mr. Edward Van Halen himself), that I purchased the previous Christmas, and amp along with my Boss Distortion, Digital Delay, and wah-wah pedals. I was set. My career would be launched that day, I was doubtless. So I got up in front of two teachers and a pair of popular students I knew who had an '80's hair-band that was playing a full concert as part of the festivities. The latter were not only dedicated, professional-quality musicians, but top athletes as well; at the pinnacle of the school's cool chain; poised to explode onto the big time once they graduated and everyone knew it.

I took the stage by storm and shredded as best I could, imaging that I was headlining at the Forum in from of 15,000 adoring, screaming fans. At last, the students of OHS would realize that I was in fact cool, and they would come to respect me; they'd come to the conclusion that they were wrong about me all the time; I'd become popular. The girls would swoon in my presence and everyone would stop laughing at me behind my back and no longer would I be called "geek" or "loser." I would show them all. I would become a King!

What I didn't realize is that I was awkward and terminally uncharismatic, and making those moves only made that fact horribly apparent. I came off more like a court jester than a King. And my playing was sub-par, to say the least. Listening to some of my practice tapes years later I realized that while my fingers were fast, I was going in and out of key and missing notes; and the fact that I didn't notice brought out another fatal flaw: I had problems with my pitch. What I should have done years earlier is buy a typewriter instead of an axe and start writing about bands rather than try to be in one.

Now was not my time, and music was not my vocation. High school, especially that one, was not a place for me to shine or show my true self. That would have to come later. I would have to be a little more patient.

When I finished my piece they politely applauded and thanked me for coming in but adroitly avoided making eye contact with me.

One of the teachers present told me a few days later that I did not make the cut when I ran into her in the hall. She tried to hold back laughter as she shook her head after I confronted her and asked if they had made their decision. I thought for sure that I had made it, and at first believed that the two popular students were jealous and trying to sabotage me. I now know they did me a big favour; if I had got up in front of the whole school and did that routine, I would have been laughed out of the building.

But that didn't faze me at the time. I still had the Vanier audition coming up. Because I studied and took the McGill courses, I aced the written part. But my audition was a bigger catastrophe than the talent show fiasco. I played power chords and solos, but the two teachers, both older, overweight men, one of whom had enough gross disgusting hair coming out of his nose that he could probably braid it; I mean, would it have killed him to trim it? They cut me off in the middle of my playing and asked me to sight read. I had just started to learn that a few months earlier and was not up to their standards.

"How long have you been playing?" Professor Nosehair asked.

"For three years, man."

"And you still haven't learned to sight read?" he said angrily, as though personally offended.

I didn't know what to say.

"You are wasting our time!" he said.

After a few seconds the other teacher thanked me and I was asked to leave. A letter of rejection came in the mail two weeks later. I was so despondent that I let my already shaky schoolwork flounder and eventually I flunked out of OHS.

I was determined that summer to get better and began practicing twice as much.

When autumn came and most of my friends were off to CEGEPs, I went to night school to make up my courses. There I met another musician who liked my chops. He was a bass player who knew another guitarist, a Hendrix clone, and wanted to start a band.

So the three of us got together for some serious jamming, one time in an apartment building's vast parking garage, which I guess made us the world's largest garage band. But after a few sessions they stopped returning my calls and I realized that I was fired.

I was at a crossroads: Keep trying and end up the rhythm guitarist in a second-rate AC/DC cover band, or give it up and move on to something else. By then I had the maturity to realize that I was infatuated with being a rock star; the supposed lifestyle and unrealistic glamour, not at being a skilled and dedicated musician. I did not regret the time I spent playing; it gave me something to do that I enjoyed. But I had to let it go.

My musical experience later helped land me my first payroll job out of university at a record store. And the two guys with the cool high school band? They never made it big either, but from what I heard they still play music professionally, although it is not necessarily their main source of income. They do it not to be stars, but because they enjoy it. But hey, at least I could say (in a way) that I sold more CD's (in my five and a half years at the record store) then they did. But I heard that one of them distributes imported Greek music now, so even that claim has become dubious.

A few years ago I was walking along de Maisonneuve on my way to meet my then girlfriend for a movie at the AMC Forum. On the corner of Lambert-Closse Street I saw my old music teacher. He was sitting on the rail outside a local greasy spoon diner casually smoking a cigarette. Dressed in a smooth all-black suit he still had the demeanour, coolness and presence of a rock star.

I turned and looked at him. We made eye contact. He didn't seem to recognize me. I was about to speak, but then I thought: *Would he remember me or would this turn into another awkward situation generated by me in which I tried to explain to someone who I was?*

I looked away, then looked back a moment later. This time he shot me a "What're you lookin' at? What's your problem?" type leer. Again I said nothing, and continued on my way.

A DAY AT THE BEACH

Montreal is world-renowned for many great things, but decent beaches are certainly not included on that list. Although an island in the St. Lawrence River, Montreal is at least a day's drive from any ocean. For relief from a scorching hot summer day in a natural body of water, a Montrealer once had to drive ninety minutes to Plattsburg, New York for a dip in the skin hive inducing waters of Lake Champlain, or the equal time to one of Eastern Ontario's many public parks. There is a beach at Oka that is fairly close, but for some reason the ground under the murky water feels like shit when you walk on it. And I mean that literally. It feels like walking barefoot on excrement.

One Saturday evening when I was about nineteen, my friend The Weasel told me that Kosta, a long-time friend of his brother Sam, was organizing a trip to an Ontario beach for the next day. We were all to meet at Kosta's family home in Ville St. Laurent for a 9 a.m. departure. While I casually knew most of the people who would be going, they were not really my crowd so I was reluctant. But as usual The Weasel, who is smoother than a baby's bottom and was quite enthusiastic about attending, nagged me into coming along.

To go I had to wake up early on Sunday, one of the seven days I usually reserve for sleeping in during the summer. The Weasel picked me up in the black Ford Mustang his father had recently helped him buy. The car was retrofitted with an obnoxiously loud stereo boom box and sound system, that we went all the way to New York City to buy on Canal Street, from which The Weasel, who has the worst taste in music of any human on this planet, blasted even more obnoxious dance club/Hip-Hop music. (The aforementioned rewired sound system ignited a fire in his glovebox while I was in the passenger seat when we were coming back from the Dairy Queen on Park Avenue about a year later; the car was damaged but soon repaired. Everyone on Wiseman Avenue poured out onto the street to see the firemen extinguish the small blaze.) His two favourites were "Baby Got Back" and "Funky Cold Medina" by a rapper called Tone Loc. He would like to play those songs at an eardrum-splitting volume with extra bass as we cruised down Ste. Catherine Street on a hot summer Friday or Saturday night. I was so embarrassed I would try to duck down so no one could see me.

"Do you know what Funky Cold Medina is?" The Weasel would ask me with a sly, impish grin.

"No idea," I answered.

"It's Spanish Fly," he said.

"Spanish what? What the fuck is that?"

"You know *ré* … Spanish Fly."

"What's that? A Hispanic zipper?"

"God, you are such a total loser," he said as though he could not understand why he was wasting his life being my friend. "Spanish Fly is something you put in a girl's drink to make her horny."

"Why would you want to do that?"

"So she would have sex with you, *ré* loser!"

"Why would you have to do *that* to get her to have sex with you?"

"God!" he said, exasperated, "what is wrong with you?"

Typical for us, we arrived at Kosta's on time and as usual most everyone was not yet there. Kosta himself was not even out of bed. The others slowly began to arrive much later.

Among the group were friends of Sam's including Carlos, a black-haired Portuguese kid with big, white buck teeth so huge their outline could be seen even when his mouth was closed, and whom I knew from my time at Outremont High School. He had a class clown sort of personality and reputation, but I just found him loud and annoying.

Also arriving was a body-builder most of Sam's friends called "The German" despite being Greek. But I called him Sven because he had the appearance of a Scandinavian with his pale white skin, fine thin blonde hair and Aryan blue eyes, although his personality and accent were pure Greek. Sven over-did the weight-lifting to the point where his head looked like a marble on top of a side of beef. He once told me about the time he ran into a local celebrity fortune teller who reminded me of Bette Davis in *What Ever Happened to Baby Jane?* and said to her as a joke that when he called her 1-976 number and got a reading, nothing she predicted had happened and he wanted his money back. Clearly Sven had a wit that would make Dorothy Parker green with envy. And I'm certain no one ever said anything like that to her before.

When he told me this, I imagined the soothsayer asking him for a dollar with the promise she'd tell him something that would absolutely come true. After giving her the money, she'd say: "No one will kick you really hard in the balls today," and then proceed to give him a hard shot in the nards with one of her stilettos. As he rolled on the ground in agony, she would toss him back his loonie and say: "Oh well, I guess I'm wrong again. Here's your refund, jerk!"

The last person to arrive was someone we all called *Psilos*, which in Greek loosely translates to "tall guy." Although he was not all that much taller than me, he was very slim and angular, making him appear to be a head above everyone else. Psilos had the reputation of being hot-headed, although he seemed like a decent guy to me and I never had a problem with him. Sam told me about one particular time when he, Psilos, Kosta, Sven, and some other guys from the neighbourhood were playing a game of Monopoly and Psilos was the first one to lose all his money. He immediately flew into a rage and stormed out of the house. When the game was over they discovered that as he left he took all their shoes and flung them out into the street; cars had been running over their footwear all night. Psilos had invited his cousin Stavros, known to us as Steve, from Laval to come along, so we had to wait for even more people to arrive. It was another hour or so until he showed, and finally we were off, three hours later than planned.

Sam did not come with us that day, for which all the boys were grateful. Despite being short, stocky, and kind of rough-looking, where it counted Sam was built like a porn star. He would strut the beach in his speedo, drawing stares and gasps from the women while putting all us guys to shame. I theorized that years ago his shlong pulled a *coup d'état* and overthrew him, so that it was in reality his dick that walked around and interacted with us, while Sam was forever trapped inside the swimwear, powerless to escape.

The reason The Weasel was so keen on going soon became clear to me: He had an interest in one of the girls coming with us that day. The

Weasel asked me not to ride with him; he wanted to be alone with her and her friend. The only reason he badgered me into going was to keep him company in case she didn't end up being there. That is why I tagged him "The Weasel," a moniker I borrowed from David Letterman, who often referred to the annoying NBC and later CBS executives who constantly interfered with his show as "those network executive Weasels." I first met The Weasel at Outremont High when we were fifteen; he was clad in skin tight bleached white jeans, a pink Lacoste shirt, leather shoes with no socks (to this day he still doesn't wear socks, even in the winter … what's wrong with him!?!); his hair was coloured a golden brown, curled on top, and gelled back on the sides. Quite a sight. And he loved listening to Madonna. He had just transferred from TMR High, which became a French-language institution, and because his cousin married Paps' cousin, we became fast friends.

Back then he had a girlfriend who went to another school, whom his mother did not care for. I resided at the time one street over and one street down from The Weasel, who hatched one of his now-famous diabolical plots to see her without getting grief from his mom. The Weasel would call and invite me over, and when I came by we would hang out for about an hour, and then we'd leave, giving his Mom the impression that we were going somewhere when in fact he was going to see his squeeze, whose mother was a single parent and often not home. (One must understand The Weasel is not like most people. On multiple occasions I bore witness to him engaging in intense bargaining sessions over miniscule amounts of money; amounts that I have seen him throw away for nothing without a hint of remorse.)

I knew what was going on, but I didn't comprehend until later why he didn't simply ask me to cover for him, which I would have gladly done: He got some sort of bizarre high from knowing that he cleverly deceived, manipulated, and/or out-manoeuvred an adversary. And all too often for him, just about everyone is an adversary.

Once on a Saturday evening before the Catholic Easter (or as I once referred to it, the *Faux* Easter) the whole gang was hanging out at The Weasel's place with nothing to do. When we disbanded late in the evening The Weasel, who didn't have a set of wheels at the time, suggested that the two of us go to Plattsburg, New York the next day in my sub-compact white Toyota Tercel hatchback. When I suggested we invite the guys, he said he preferred it be just us. So we went the next day, dined at Pizza Hut, bought American cigarettes, twinkies and six-packs of Mountain Dew (all things unavailable in Quebec at the time) and hopped back over the border. When Johnny A. found out we did that, he confronted The Weasel who claimed I said that I was afraid Johnny A., a heavy-set guy, would damage my car's springs. Of course he bought it, and would not speak to me for several months.

That style turned almost tragic a decade and a half later when The Weasel was managing a bank branch and one of his employees, who was breaking up with his live-in girlfriend, asked him if he knew anyone who would take his dog. The Weasel immediately called me and asked if I was interested. Isabella had just died a few years earlier and I wasn't ready to fall in love again, so I turned him down. When he insisted, I made it clear and in no uncertain terms that I was *not going to take the dog*!

About a month later The Employee called me and asked when he could bring over the dog.

"I told (The Weasel) I was not going to take the dog," I said.

"But he said you would," The Employee said, whimpering.

"I don't know and don't care what he told you. I told him clearly that I was not taking the dog. Sorry."

"But he said …"

"I am not going any further with this. Sorry I can't help you. This conversation is over. Good-bye!" I said and abruptly hung up the phone. I wasn't angry at The Employee. It wasn't his fault he was lied to. I was pissed at The Weasel for forcing me into another unnecessarily awkward situation.

The Employee called The Weasel right after and related to him what happened.

"Well, Andre said to me he'd take the dog," he said. "I guess he just changed his mind."

Weasel!

There were about six cars and twenty or so people in our little caravan. I rode shotgun with Kosta in his late-model two-tone Oldsmobile coupe with Psilos in the back seat, while Carlos rode in the front passenger seat of Sven's motorized vehicle, also a late-model GM coupe, in his case a grey Buick.

Of course we had to race and otherwise drive wildly all the way there. At one point when Kosta blew past Sven's car we mooned them. In retaliation Sven pulled ahead of us and Carlos stuck his entire upper torso out the passenger-side window of the car while going over 140 kph. Sven never cleaned the interior of his automobile, so Carlos had plenty of ammo to rain down on us; the damn fool started throwing Kleenex, cans, paper towels, razor blades (yes, there were actual razor blades in the car and yes, he threw them at us!) and whatever else he could get his hands on.

In the confusion, we missed the exit to the lake and got lost, which angered Psilos, who felt that Carlos' antics were responsible. The convoy pulled over to the shoulder to get our bearings. Our car had hardly stopped before Psilos started aggressively pushing and yelling: "Let me out! Let me out of the fucking car!" When I opened the door he didn't give me a chance to egress, squeezing me under the forward folding seat as he forced his way out and charged directly at Carlos, exclaiming: "Carlos! Fucking Bugs Bunny!" who just stood there with a confused look on his face as Psilos tackled him to the ground. It took five guys to finally pull Psilos off of him. I was not one of them.

Once the gang cooled down, we consulted a map and were on our way again, finally arriving at our destination at around 2 p.m. By then all the good parking spaces were gone so we had to park at an adjacent lot and hire a native guide to find our way to the beach. The good picnic tables were spoken for, but we eventually found some rotting, decrepit, Black Widow spider-infested ones near a set of overflowing, pungent, wasp-riddled garbage cans that were so far from the lake we needed binoculars to see the water.

I noticed that The Weasel was no longer talking to the girl he liked.

"What happened with her?" I asked him.

"Two minutes into the drive she started talking about a guy she has a crush on and asked me to find out if he likes her."

"So, who's the lucky guy? Is it me?"

"No," said The Weasel.

Of course not. It was never me.

"She likes Carlos," he said.

"Carlos!"

"Yup."

"Fucking Bugs Bunny!" I said.

That summer The Weasel had acquired a new baseball glove, so he gave me his old one, which was still in excellent condition. We had brought said gloves and a ball, and played catch for a while. Afterwards we took a dip in the cold, still, lifeless, mossy lake. For someone whose body evolved to walk barefoot along the Mediterranean, swamp-like Canadian inland lakes represent quite a disappointment.

We were lying on our towels back at the picnic table soaking up some rays, when Psilos and Steve approached us. They wanted to borrow our gloves for a game of catch. We had no objection.

They threw to each other, and after a few minutes Steve tossed a line drive way over Psilos' head; he jumped to catch the ball, but fell way short. It sailed away in a smooth arc down a hill, where after a few bounces it struck a young girl, who started to cry.

One of two things had happened: Either Steve threw it high on purpose to make Psilos look silly chasing it down, giving Steve something to openly ridicule him for; or it was thrown high by accident and Steve immediately covered up his own error by loudly blaming Psilos first. I think it was the latter

"You hit a girl, you loser! Why did you throw it so high, *ré*?" Psilos said.

"It's not my fault, *ré*, you can't catch!" Steve replied.

"You hit a girl, *ré malaka*! She's crying!" Psilos said.

"Hey! You jerks hurt her!" the girl's mother shouted.

"Well, next time I'll throw it harder!" Steve responded, laughing.

Steve, like all too many Greeks, saw apologizing or admitting fault or culpability as a sign of weakness, as if doing so means that one's genitalia would automatically drop off. People like him view *Anglaisos* culture as pathetic and anaemic because they are often polite and respectful to their fellow humans and say things like "sorry" or "excuse me" after unintentionally doing harm to another.

The mother, a middle-aged woman with short blonde hair and clad in a purple one-piece bathing suit and flip-flops, charged up the hill with determination towards Steve.

"She's really hurt, you sonnova bitch! You owe her an apology!" she said slapping Steve violently and shoving him to the ground.

Nobody in our group laughed or intervened. We just stood and stared at the pathetic display.

"Okay! Okay! I'm sorry!" Steve said. "I'm sorry, okay? Lemmie alone, okay! I'm sorry!"

By then I'd had it with this group. I discreetly took back my glove and ball, and packed my bag.

"C'mon," I said to The Weasel, "let's get the fuck out of here."

The Weasel had also seen enough and we quietly slipped away to his car without as much as waving goodbye to the others.

It wasn't until we were well on our way down the road home that I finally broke the silence.

I said: "If there's ever another outing with these guys, don't bother calling me."

"Don't worry. I won't … what the fuck!?!"

An indicator light on the Mustang's dashboard warned that the car was overheating. The Weasel quickly pulled over to the side of the highway and popped the hood. We looked over the engine and found that a large paper towel Carlos had thrown out of Sven's car had been sucked up by the engine and somehow lodged itself on his radiator, obstructing the airflow.

The Weasel slowly reached down, carefully peeled it off, and held it up in amazement.

"Carlos!" he said. "Fucking Bugs Bunny!"

PLAYING THE SLOTS

At Dawson College I had a drinking buddy named Arnold. He was rather fond of saying that a good pool player was indicative of a wasted youth. Once, after beating me quite soundly at a game of billiards, he asked how I had wasted my youth, because I obviously hadn't spent it in seedy pool halls like he did growing up in Chateauguay.

I told him that I in fact did shoot pool quite often when I was about sixteen with my crew that consisted of Johnny A., Stretch, Paps, The Weasel and Big Jerry. We were a close-knit bunch, and they were the only things that made the Purgatory that was Outremont High School bearable.

We were a group of unpopular guys, rejects from various other cool gangs. The real character among us was Stretch, someone with a heart of gold who would give a total stranger the shirt off his back. He enjoyed pointing finger guns at people he liked, clicking and winking as he dropped his thumb like a hammer; a sign you were okay with him, what we called the "Stretch Salute." But if he used both hands and gave you two guns, well then you were *really* down with him … I never got two guns. Stretch was the kind of guy who fancied himself a ladies' man. If a female gave him even the slightest glance he would go: "Oh, yeah! She wants me!" Hell, if he was having a heart attack and the paramedic who revived him was a woman, his first words after coming to would be: "Hey baby, what's your number?" If a fireman pulled him from a burning building, I suppose his reaction would be: "Whoa, bro! Put me down! Sorry, I'm not that way!"

We were all at the McDonald's in Old Montreal one evening. Stretch was the last to order and get his food, and when he arrived at our table upstairs he seemed overly excited.

"Guys!" he said. "I didn't have to pay for my food. The girl behind the counter, she didn't ask me to pay. She likes me! She gave me 'the look!' I'm gonna go down after and ask her out! Oh yeah, I'm the man!"

"How do you know it wasn't an accident?"

"C'mon, bro, I said she gave me 'the look' ... y'know, flirted with her eyes. Oh, yeah, she wants me!"

A few moments later the counter girl in question came up with the shift manager and pointed out Stretch to her. The manager approached him and sternly but politely and demanded that he pay for his meal. I'd never seen Stretch so humbled and embarrassed. We rode him about that all night.

We would spend every Friday immediately after school at a sleazy dive cappuccino shop on Bernard Street neat St. Urbain that had two pool tables. In fact it was so low class it didn't even have a name. We called the joint *Fat Gino's* because the overweight, unshaven owner was a guy who looked like he should be named Gino.

Every Friday we'd play and on Monday in homeroom I'd compile the stats and winning percentages with Big Jerry, who was two years older than us and hearing-impaired but a solid athlete and pool player, for what we referred to as the W.P.A., or World Pool Association, the "world" in question being the six of us. We had a champion and if someone were to beat him they would be the new champ. The honour sometimes changed hands several times a session, but it was never won by me, and I was usually at the bottom of the weekly rankings. I never got above .500.

When we turned seventeen in our final year of high school, we would have a unique Friday night ritual. At about 7 p.m. we'd go to for supper at a Chinese buffet on Van Horne Avenue, and then go downtown and hit the arcades, being too young for bars.

During part of my youth the City of Montreal, in its infinite wisdom, banned anyone under eighteen from the amusement arcades. At the time I couldn't understand why, but it was a royal pain, and to me it made no sense. I mean, who else but hopelessly undatable and terminally uncool minors would waste so much time and money at a place like that? At the time the movie rating system banned those under fourteen or eighteen from the cooler movies, so what else could we do?

In Grade 6, during a day off from school, my cousin Christos and I walked up Ste. Catherine Street from Atwater to Bleury looking for arcades that would let us play. We'd walk into a joint and ask someone from the staff if they allowed minors, and were immediately shown the door. A guy once pointed out the exit before I even had a chance to ask him if we could play there. We were thrown out of every one. Looking back now, I should be grateful. My father was right; those places were a colossal waste of time. On occasion there would be a greasy spoon diner, pizza parlour, or *dépanneur* somewhere with an old pinball machine or a few games where the owner turned a blind eye to under-aged players, but that was about it.

The ban was lifted when I was in my mid-teens, so me and my crew spent our dateless Fridays defending the earth from invaders, re-fighting World War II, or trying to outrace our competitors.

We would sometimes come across others of our kind from OHS. Once we ran into a kid we knew named Ishvalan. He was one of the smart, science class nerds and was heavily into arcade games. Ish even knew how to fix the games with a quarter on a string, and got us some free plays. That particular establishment's owner was a 300-pound Goliath who looked like he was thrown out of a biker gang for been *too* mean, as Ish was quick to point out, adding: "He looks like the kind of guy who gives the kids he catches fixing the games a sound beating. Well, enjoy guys!" as he moved on to the next machine, setting up free plays for anyone who wanted. I didn't see him playing all that often. He must have been some sort of arcade anarchist, and was doing it for the principle, to upset the system, or to fight the power, or just because he could.

Mean-looking, biker types were sometimes a necessity, because they could be rough places. (Hmm … maybe *that's* why they banned minors?) One evening, at the Alexis Nihon Plaza arcade, Johnny A. was playing pinball while right next to him a couple of toughs were slapping around some other kid for his quarters. At one point the assailants were banging their victim's head on the side of the machine Johnny A. was using. He decided not to get involved, but strangely enough didn't walk away from the scene, either. He just kept his head down as low as possible with eyes on the playfield and kept on going, setting a new highest score in the process.

We'd usually cruise several establishments in an evening, depending on which games we wanted to play or how busy they were. On a fateful evening we went to the arcade on St. Paul Street in Old Montreal and had an epiphany.

At the time the most realistic racing simulator was a Formula 1 style game called *Final Lap*. It was fun to play, but only had seats for two people at a time. However at the Old Montreal arcade they didn't have two, or three, but four *Final Lap* machines. And they were wired together so eight (yes ... *eight!*) people could race against each other simultaneously. It was like discovering a new element! From then on, we only went to that arcade, and only played that game, greedily hogging it for hours. Each of us would get a roll or two of quarters sit down and race each other until our coins were exhausted and our sweaty hands had to be pried off the steering wheels with a Jaws of Life.

Johnny A. and Stretch had an especially fierce rivalry. I was never as good as they were at that game; for me the greatest victory in a field of eight was making it to the podium, or if not that then just to not be last. Often they would sit side by side and try to cut the other off or run the other off the road. When Johnny A. proved the victor, Stretch would cry out: "I'll get you next time, you fat slob!" So loud the whole place would hear. (No small feat given how noisy those establishments could be.) But it was courtesy of their intense desire to defeat one another that I won my first race.

On the ultimate lap of that particular race I was running a strong 3rd place. Just ahead of me were Johnny A. and Stretch. I could see them violently battling for the lead. They kept aggressively bumping each other, determined to triumph, and eventually they pushed each other off the track on the last turn and I sailed through to an easy victory.

There was another night when Johnny A. did not win any of the races, which really pissed him off. We all agreed to go back the next evening and play again. And when we did Johnny A. didn't finish lower than 2nd, and won two-thirds of the time. We later discovered he had gotten up early that morning, went to Old Montreal and spent a substantial amount of money at the arcade practicing.

We had a gentleman's agreement not to tell anyone else about our discovery. *Final Lap* was the hottest racing game of the day, and if word got out about the four linked games at the St. Paul Street arcade, which was away from the usual circuit and frequented mostly by tourists, we would have to wait like losers to use the game. Then it happened.

Johnny A. showed up at my front door one Saturday morning with a copy of *The Gazette*. In the entertainment section was a large advertisement that read: "Play *Final Lap* with a bunch of your friends! We have four games linked together!" Or something stupid like that. The asshole owner of the arcade must've put that ad in the French language papers as well, because that evening the place was jammed with gamers. We didn't get anywhere near a chance to play all night. We all knew it was too good to last.

After a while, we started college, got jobs and girlfriends and had no more free time to spend at those places.

Eventually things like PlayStation and Nintendo wiped out most of the old arcades. Now all the flashy, loud spots that used to dot Ste. Catherine Street have become boutiques and cheap restaurants; peepshow palaces and strip joints and massage parlours. Sure, there are still a few left, but I don't go in anymore.

I stroll over to the video games at the movie theatre sometimes, but they look so large (some of them a bigger than my car), loud, fast and complicated I dare not chance a quarter, or whatever they cost now. I would probably be embarrassingly bad at them anyway. I do occasionally play the pinball machines. I was pretty okay at that when I was young. It's refreshing to see yet another classic that has stood the test of time.

These days, when I look at the kids playing the slots and the machines with their over-the-top sounds and flashing lights, I have mixed emotions. Did I waste my time and money in arcades? Hell yeah! Would I give up any of my memories? Hell no!

When you think about it, who among us hasn't wasted at least part of their youth?

THE SEER

I am not a believer in the paranormal or supernatural. I don't claim to know the nature of existence, but I'm pretty sure the universe will never be deciphered by a deck of tarot cards or in the entrails of an owl. When I was younger, because of the influence of my mother and some of my friends, I flirted with superstitions, but I slowly outgrew the habit. While I do practice some minor, insignificant personal rituals, I try not to delude myself into thinking that fate can be controlled by carrying around part of a dead animal or avoiding cracks in the sidewalk; they are more a habit than anything else. As for those who say they know all the answers because they claim to have some kind of divine power, I am completely aware that they are hucksters and charlatans.

There was, however, an instance where I did pay a visit to a fortune teller. And as usual, the story involves a girl.

Her name was Cheryl. We were students in Dawson College's Creative Arts program. I was a rocker geek, and she was the hottest thing in the solar system that the Earth did not revolve around. With her long, light-brown hair teased to perfection, she was a half-Italian, half-Polish bombshell; a hard rock goddess with a curvaceous, voluptuous body poured into a Led Zeppelin T-shirt, skin-tight jeans, and brown suede vest with matching tasselled cowboy boots, belt and purse. She cruised the halls of Dawson with the confident, slick, slow, smooth saunter of an old west gunslinger, turning heads and breaking hearts.

Cheryl was a well-connected party girl and rock groupie who liked to hang with musicians and drug dealers. She once told me she had sex with David Lee Roth, (I didn't know if she was having me on or not; I think she likely she was just pulling my leg to see how gullible I was). I had heard from others that she often got herself backstage at big-time rock shows at the Forum with little effort, but I have no first-hand knowledge of any of this. For instance, one of our classmates with whom she was good friends claimed Cheryl was able to procure a pair of hard plastic "All Access" passes and they got to meet Robert Plant at an after show party. When I asked how she acquired them, he simply said she "knew some people."

I was barely a blip on her radar, but not too enamoured to realize that she'd never go out with me even if I headlined at The Forum. Regardless I gave it my best shot.

Whenever I'd run into Cheryl in the cafeteria, I would park myself next to her, and because we liked the same kind of music and I played guitar, at minimum we had a few things in common to talk about. One day I sat next to her as she was talking to some girls from our television production class.

"Hey Adonis," she said to me.

She never got my name right. Once in the same conversation she called me both "Angelo" and "Anthony."

"I was just telling everyone about this fortune teller I just went to named Mrs. Melina. She was incredible. You should all go see her!"

"Sure, I'd love to," I said with enthusiasm. "How do I do that?"

Of course the only reason I wanted to go was so that I could have another excuse to talk to Cheryl. I telephoned the number she gave me the moment I got home and made an appointment to see Mrs. Melina for the following Saturday. What sounded like a young girl took the call, and gave me instructions on how to get to the house. The session would cost $20, cash only. She would, however, not let me talk to Mrs. Melina, saying she didn't like to speak on phones.

Was she afraid her line was tapped?

I showed up that Saturday a half hour before my appointment. The house was just your average N.D.G. duplex row-house near the Vendôme metro just off of Upper Lachine Road. Nothing special. I rang the bell and waited for about a minute before someone answered.

The front door slowly swung open to reveal a pair of pre-teen twins with light blue eyes and brown hair combed the exact same way. While not dressed in the same colours, they were clad in similar sweatshirts and jeans.

"Ah, hello," I said.

They just stood there, silently staring at me.

"My name is Andreas. I'm here to see Mrs. Melina."

Still nothing.

"Am I at the right house?"

They looked at each other for a second, then back at me. Finally one of them said: "You're early."

"Ah, yes, I know. Please excuse me. I miscalculated how long it would take to get here. I don't usually come out to N.D.G. by bus and metro, you see ... Ah, is she available?"

After a long, awkward pause, the other twin said: "We'll see if she can take you now. Please come in."

I cautiously entered the house to find its interior very inconspicuous. No creepy taxidermy or talismans in sight. The flat contained typical hardwood floors and a long hallway that connected to most of the rooms. I followed one of the twins to a small, undecorated chamber that was little more than a glorified passageway from one larger room to another. The only furniture was a small wooden table with two chairs, like the kind we had at school, both of which were situated on one side.

On the table were two sets of cards: One thick deck with a blue and white diamond pattern on the back; the others were thinner, black and quite well-worn.

"Just have a seat, and put the $20 on the table," she said. "My sister will bring Mrs. Melina when she's ready."

I thanked her and did what she said. After a few minutes of twiddling my thumbs, the room's other door slowly creaked open, and out came a wheelchair pushed by one of the twins, who rolled its occupant to the table, making sure she was facing me. She locked the wheelchair, and then quickly exited the room, shutting the door behind her.

"Mrs. Melina, I presume," I said.

"Yes," she answered in a pronounced Italian accent.

"Sorry I'm early, but I guess you knew I'd be early, didn't you?"

"What? Why would I know that?" she said with a confused look.

"Nothing. Forget it," I quickly said.

Mrs. Melina was clad in the kind of black dress preferred by Greek or Italian widows. Her two front teeth were oversized, a faded off-white, and crooked. Her graying hair was tied back into a tight bun.

She definitely bore some kind of illness. Her entire body appeared paralysed and shrivelled. The only thing she was capable of moving was her right arm. However, her right hand remained locked in a curled-up state and resembled a barbed hook. She had very long, sharp-looking fingernails. Although it was likely polio, I never found out what she suffered from. I spend most of the session hoping my vaccinations were up to date.

She asked if I had trouble finding the house and made small talk while awkwardly trying to shuffle the cards with her only good limb.

"Do you want me to do that for you?" I asked, trying to be helpful.

"No!" she burst out, waving her hook hand in my face. "I have to do this or it will not work! You do not touch the cards or there could be dire consequences!"

She must have learned that move from the blackjack dealers in Atlantic City.

Just then another scary thought hit me: Nobody knew I was there. I had her phone number and address on a piece of paper in my pocket, and the only person I told about this couldn't even remember my name. Mrs. Melina could just push a button under the table and I would drop though the floor and into a dungeon where she kept young men to feed on their brains in order to regain her motor functions. Hell, I was afraid she'd have a conniption and wildly swing that jagged hand, jamming it into my jugular and opening up a gusher for the creepy twins to feast on.

But none of those things happened. We just continued the session. She first shuffled the blue and white cards and asked me point out a number of them. She then proceeded to tell me my fortune based on what she saw in the cards. We talked about many personal but inconsequential things, like my relationships with women or my parents; most of it on a superficial level but unlike Cheryl and probably most of Mrs. Melina's clients, there was never a "wow!" moment where she exactly nailed something about me. To be honest I can hardly recall anything she told me. I later found most of her clients take notes, but I didn't know that was permitted.

Then she asked me to choose several cards from the black deck. All I remember is that that one of the cards I selected was referred to excitedly by Mrs. Melina as the "card of destiny, the best card of the deck to pick!"

So at least I have that going for me.

After the session I thanked her and left. While departing I saw her next appointment waiting on a couch in the living room. He was a very well dressed, middle-aged businessman-type in a brown suit with a big moustache and glasses who didn't look like someone needing reassurance or spiritual guidance.

Perhaps he was also trying to score with Cheryl?

On my way out I passed one of the twins' bedroom, and caught a glimpse of her through the wide open door lying on top of her bed and gabbing on the phone like a regular teeny-bopper about the latest hunky teen idol, using terms like "totally" and "omigod, what-*ever!*" Suddenly she didn't seem so creepy anymore.

The following Monday I looked for Cheryl in the cafeteria so that I could tell her about my visit to Mrs. Melina. I entirely believed she would be anxious to hear the story. I sat next to her as she was talking to several others.

"Hello Alexis," she said.

Okay now she just doing that on purpose! Who did she think I was? Zorba?

"Hey, Cheryl! Guess what? I saw Mrs. Melina last Saturday."

"Oh, did I tell you about her?" she said. "Good. I hope you had fun." She quickly turned away from me and continued on with the others at her table as if I were invisible.

I felt like a damn fool. But that didn't stop me.

Not long after I finally gathered the courage to ask Cheryl out. She turned me down flat. When I asked her why, she said: "Well, you're only 19; just a teenager."

"You're 20! Only a few months older than me."

"Yeah, but we're too different; I'm a child of the '60's, and you're a '70's guy."

"What do you mean? You were born in October 1969, and I was born in January 1970. Once again only a few months apart. And in two days we'll be the same age!"

"We'll never be the same age," she said. "But anyway, you still live at home."

"What are you talking about? Almost everyone I know my age still lives at home! At nineteen that's no disgrace!"

"Well I've been on my own since I was sixteen."

True, when she was sixteen she left her parents to run off with a drug dealer, and for whatever reason, likely because it is possible her old-school European parents themselves got married as teenagers, they had no objection. Said drug dealer, on more than one occasion, beat her savagely, once going so far as to fracture her skull. That was the point when she decided to leave him. And she did ... eventually. (So for her a woman-beating felon was good enough but I somehow couldn't quite make the cut.)

A decade later I had a girlfriend who, when she was a teenager, saved up all her money from years of working at McDonald's, and left home on her eighteenth birthday to flee an oppressive father, choosing to live alone in a one-room rat-hole in Verdun. Her only furniture was a mattress on the floor. *That's* a strong, independent woman.

My own mother left her improvised home at seventeen, two years after her father died, to go live in Athens. She went around looking for work, but was often ridiculed for her *Vlahos* (bumpkin hick) accent. Whenever she found work she sent what she could home to her mother. Mom lived at a boarding house with a group of artists, musicians and actors until she finally came to Canada in 1960 as a domestic worker. A few years later she earned her citizenship, and brought over all her siblings, most of whom started businesses and otherwise prospered in the New World; they had children, who had children of their own – just think of how many Canadians are now here because my Mom immigrated – and how many future generations will arise because of one brave woman looking for a better life. A woman raised two teenagers as a single mom in a community of busybodies who would whisper malicious gossip about her because she got a divorce. *That's* a strong, independent woman.

Cheryl never had a minimum wage job with a paper hat and plastic name tag. The only work she did was as a model and drug mule.

I don't know what happened to Cheryl. She wanted to become an actress, and I heard she had moved to Toronto after graduation to pursue that goal, but to date I've never seen her in any movie or televised broadcast.

And all I really got for my $20 was yet another story to tell about the crazy things I've done to win a woman's heart.

"YOUR DRIVER'S LICENSE, YOU INFIDEL DOG!"

When I was at Concordia I lived in an apartment my brother leased in Snowdon, close to the Loyola campus. I moved there when his roommate left to join the army. The price was right, and my mother had remarried and I didn't want to live with her and her new husband, so it was almost ideal. But there was one slight drawback: I had no job and no steady source of income. Tuition and books were not a problem, but there was rent and groceries and other assorted bills that oddly enough came around every month.

As a teenager I had two jobs: part-time at an ice factory when I was fifteen and part-time at a bakery when I was sixteen, both just for the summer and I was glad when they were over. When I was seventeen I started working as an extra in film and TV. It was infrequent but it paid well. I also did odd jobs around the neighbourhood and worked from time to time for the mother of a friend who had a clothing business, and I liked it that way; end of the day I had the money in my hand. But now if I were to keep up my end of the apartment I had to get a payroll job.

I returned from classes one Friday afternoon to find my brother and his girlfriend Annick, who was the assistant manager at a self-serve gas station in Côte-des-Neiges, sitting at the kitchen table, and they were both glad to see me.

"Guess what?" Peter said. "They just fired the nighttime weekend guy at the station and they need a replacement. Annick says you're hired. You start tonight working from 11 p.m. to 7 a.m."

That was it. No interview. No screening. I started that night.

I continued with the company for almost two years at three different stations, none of which were in the nicest areas.

One gloomy afternoon I was working the station at St. Jacques near Cavendish when two cars, both BMW's, simultaneously pulled up to neighbouring pumps, one driven by a middle-aged woman, the other by an older man. The woman stayed in the car when the man got out and pumped exactly 15 litres of gas into her car, and then from another pump exactly 25 litres into his as she drove off. I knew right away he had confused the volume gage with the price (a common occurrence with those pumps, which to be fair was easy to do). Gasoline was about 70¢ a litre at the time so his bill came to about $28. He marched into the kiosk and practically threw two $20 bills at me and left. When I realized his mistake I immediately made his change and ran out to give it to him and explain what he'd done wrong. By then he was already in his car and about to drive away.

"Sir!" I said. "Sir! Please wait! You gave me too much …"

"What!?! I put $15 in one car and $25 in another. That makes $40! What are you, an idiot!?!" he growled at me, believing that I was unaware of the other car.

I froze for a second and contemplated this moral dilemma?

Should I tell him about his mistake, or keep the money?

"You understand now, you moron?" he said.

That settles it!

"Yes … yes I do … sorry to bother you," I said.

"Good," he said with a degree of satisfaction as he sped off with his money in my hands and too little fuel in his tank. Back then $12 was enough for two packs of cigarettes and a chocolate bar. And that's what I used it for. At the time I had to over work two hours to get that much so I considered it a bonus.

One of the things I liked about the job was its flexibility and the fact that the manager was not there most days, and during my weekend/night shifts I didn't see the boss at all. So once I cleaned the kiosk and the bathroom, I could do what I wanted while waiting for customers. I read almost all of *Wacousta* at the station. At one point I worked a 3 p.m. to 11 p.m. Saturday shift, then a 7 a.m. to 3 p.m. Sunday shift. In between I would get some drive thru, sleep for about four hours, then go back to work, usually ordering breakfast from Picasso's restaurant. While I sacrificed my weekend, at least all my work for the week was over in 24 hours.

Besides selling gas we also sold cigarettes, and most of the Côte-des-Neiges customers at 4 a.m. were hookers, junkies, dirt-bags or lowlifes. Fortunately they mostly kept to themselves and were in and out as fast as possible, probably staying one step ahead of the cops they imagined were always after them. I got to meet quite a few strange characters and interesting people, especially working overnight. But I never thought I would encounter someone who would change my perception of an entire people.

One night a taxi driver entered the kiosque to pay for his gas and buy a pack of cigarettes. He worked for Champlain Taxi, the same predominantly Greek company as my father, and he looked Greek, so I greeted him in Greek. He didn't understand me, but he knew what was up.

"Sorry, I am not Greek. I am Iranian. Persian."

I asked him if he knew my father, but he didn't. There was no real surprise. My father worked days in the Park Extension area, and this guy spent most of his time working nights either in Côte-Des-Neiges or downtown. He left after paying and I didn't see him again for a few weeks.

The next time I saw him I noticed he was wearing a military style belt.

"Were you in the army in Iran?" I asked, wondering if he were a veteran of the bloody Iran/Iraq war of the 80's.

"No, I was police officer," he said with a friendly smile. "Iranian Highway Patrol."

Iranian Highway Patrol?

Then it hit me. Why shouldn't Iran have a highway patrol? Their roads need policing too, don't they? But because the only thing at the time I heard about Iran in the news is how they hate The West and how they cut off the hands of thieves or want to make nuclear weapons, or when there's some sort of radical anti-American protest, certain things did not occur to me.

I never even imagined that Iran had a highway patrol that did not enforce Islamic law (I've never read the Koran, but I'm pretty sure there's nothing in it about highway safety and rules for operating a motorized vehicle), but rather issues tickets for speeding, or not wearing seatbelts. And if someone violates those laws, they are not stoned to death, beheaded or dismembered, but required to pay a fine, relinquish their licence, or pay higher insurance rates.

We never see in the news anything about how old you have to be to drive in Iran (until the end of Anthony Bourdain's *Parts Unknown* when he visited the Islamic Republic), or what their speed limits are, or the level of difficulty of their driving tests. The people over there have to wait in line at the motor vehicle departments to have their licence picture taken, or their plates renewed, just like us. They have to go to driver's school and take tests like everyone else. Their teenagers have to ask for the keys to the family car so they could hang out with friends or go see a movie as do ours.

That was not long after the first Gulf War and at the time the airwaves were flooded with propaganda about Iranians that essentially painted them as people who only acted based on the Koran and spent every moment of their lives doing little else. The Western media would shock, horror and frighten us with images of an Iran where they teach the Koran in public schools, and make children recite "Death to America!" Meanwhile the very same media has no serious problem with prayer and Bible class in American schools or something as ridiculous as *Intelligent Design* being taught. The only difference I can perceive is which way the respective holy texts open.

I have never been a big fan of religion, best exemplified by the time I was going to be Best Man at The Weasel's wedding. After the rehearsal an administrator from the church took us all into her office. She was a small woman in her 60's who spoke with a thick Greek accent.

"Okay," she said as she pointed at me, "*eef* you are going to be *kubaros* [the Greek version of a 'best man'], you have to *djoin* the *tserts*."

"I don't want to join your stupid church," I said.

The Weasel bowed his head in manner that said: "Oh no, not again with this guy!"

"My friend is already paying you a shitload of money to have this wedding here, and now you want to squeeze us for more?" I said. "What are you? The Mafia?"

I flashed back to when I was sixteen and I said to some of the guys in gym class that I didn't believe in God. One of them, an obnoxious loudmouth named Nektarios who looked like a bespectacled human/ewok hybrid, burst into a fervor and spouted at me a series of machine-gun fast clichéd old religious lines of rhetoric in Greek that featured the word "*Xristos*" and "*Theos*" while hissing, spitting, waving his arms and otherwise carrying on like a raving lunatic. When he ran out of bullshit he shook his finger in my face and said that I was crazy. So he does all this, and believes things like the world was flooded and all animals were saved on an ark, or someone died and came back to life three days later, and *I'm* the insane one. *I'm* the one who needs help. Right. But most of the kids in the class sided with him. Serves me right for thinking gym class at Outremont High School was the proper place for an intelligent theological discussion.

But The Administrator was surprisingly diplomatic, especially given my lack of tact.

"Look," she said without raising her voice or losing her composure, "*eet eez* a *tserts*, but *eet eez* a *beeziness* too."

That was a refreshing admission. I appreciated that she didn't try to insult my intelligence. So much so that I was not sure what to say next. I was about to open my mouth when The Weasel, ever the keen negotiator, intervened.

"Look Andre, I will pay the membership fee and then after a year you just let it lapse."

I came to my senses and, despite not agreeing with that in principle, I realized that it wasn't about me and my friend's wedding was more important than proving a point that would be lost on everyone. So I agreed, and for the first and last time ever I spent a year as a member of a Greek Orthodox Church. They sent me a monthly newsletter, which I threw away without ever opening, and after twelve months I was again officially a person without faith. And quite happy to be so.

Are you afraid of the idea of Iran having a nuclear weapon? I am. But to be fair, I am afraid of any nation, including my own, possessing such horrible weapons. It scares me that the U.S.A. has weapons of mass destruction and the men who control them claim to be quite religious, and use examples from some anachronistic, outdated so-called holy book to guide how they govern their land and pass laws. But what horrifies me most of all is that Christianity is essentially a doomsday cult with its most ardent followers anxiously awaiting the return of the Messiah, and the apocalypse that will ensue. And why are they looking forward to this? Because it is written that all true believers will pass unto the Kingdom of Heaven. This seems okay to them, wanting the world to come to an end, and everyone in the world dying and all that, yet we call a suicide bomber crazy because he believes he'll get a shitload of virgins in Paradise?

To me, this does not make sense. How is one better than the other? And who is more frightening? A small country in Asia with a couple of crappy nuclear reactors or the world's largest and only real superpower with enough nuclear weapons to annihilate us all, and the men controlling it making decisions from an ancient book of fairy tales? America can wipe Iran off the map using one Vanguard-class nuclear submarine parked in the Indian Ocean and once they start there is nothing the Iranians can do to stop it. Who should fear whom?

Maybe it's only rhetoric, but why can't it be rhetoric from both sides? Why does one have to be good, and the other evil? Can't they both be wrong? Or right? Or good? Or evil?

And as all of this is going on, along some lonely stretch of highway sits a police officer in his patrol car with a radar gun hoping to catch a speeder and make his quota of tickets. As that officer waits, possibly contemplating what to do for their upcoming child's birthday, or where to go for vacation, does it really matter what highway it is? And which country?

SWEET JUDY BLUE-EYE

Marie-France was an esthetician who worked in a beauty salon at the other end of the mall from the record store where I was employed. She would come by two or three times a month, mostly to browse, but it was not uncommon for her to by an occasional CD or movie. She was a Carol Burnett type and had a friendly, bubbly personality. I called her "Doctor" because she was always clad in a white lab coat; we had a good rapport.

The last time Marie-France came to my shop she was more than six months pregnant and soon to go on maternity leave. I was glad she came by that evening because I was dying to ask her about a new employee at her salon. She was about my age and had short, black hair. She reminded me of Isabella Rossellini. I wanted to do a background check to see if she had a boyfriend or whatever.

"Oh, her!" Marie-France said, enthusiastically, "No, she's not seeing anyone. You know what, I think you two would go great together. I'll see if she is interested when I get back to work."

That was way beyond what I had hoped for. Not only was she available, but I had someone on the inside helping me out. For the next half hour I was walking on air.

Finally Marie-France returned, looking serious. I had a feeling the answer was "no." I went up to her and she spoke before I could inquire. What she said next I did not expect.

"Look, I should've talked straight with you before. She's married."

"Married?" I said. "And you knew this all along?"

"Yeah she married some rich guy twice her age who lives around here. She's some kind of mail-order trophy wife from Russia or something like that. Sorry."

I didn't know what bothered me more: That she was married or that Marie-France lied to me for no real reason. Was she trying to make me feel like a chump? Why would anyone do that?

"Are you okay?" she asked me.

"Yeah, I'm okay," I said.

"Are we cool?" she asked.

"Yeah. Everything's cool," I answered, "no problem."

"Sorry," Marie-France repeated, and they she walked away. I never saw her again. She was probably too embarrassed to ever come back.

* * *

I can remember the first time I saw Judy. She was wearing Capri jeans, which showed off her smooth, perfectly formed calves, and canvas sneakers; her blemish-free alabaster skin was a bit more pinkish than pale; her auburn hair was cut in a stylish mushroom, with one of the bangs so long it obscured her right eye; her left eye a soft powder blue. Her ears were long, and one of her front teeth was askew, but that only added to her charm; she totally rocked that look. On top of that she spoke with a refined English accent and had a strong, care-free, independent demeanour unlike anyone else I had ever met; with a maturity and confidence way beyond her nineteen years, she even had a large, red rose tattooed on her upper left chest. Because of her looks and outgoing personality all the boys chased after her. And for the same reason most of the girls resented her.

I was in my first full year of university, majoring in Communications after transferring from English Lit. Being a couple of years older than most of the other students in my new department, a significant portion of whom came from middle-class backgrounds, I had a difficult time fitting in socially. But I was used to that by then.

At first I resented Judy; her accent made her appear a little snobbish and when I spoke to her she seemed to dislike me. The ice was finally broken a few weeks later when we were paired together by our professor for a team project. I made some kind of smart-ass comment about her right eye being covered by her bangs, and she pulled the hair away to reveal the scarred remnants of her iris. Apparently as a child while playing with neighbour-hood children she fell into a thorn bush and the eye was badly damaged. She had limited vision and cut her hair that way to hide her disfigurement. I, of course, felt like a class A-One jerk and apologized profusely. She just shrugged it off, said it was okay, and took no offense. That's when I did a complete 180 and really started to like her; we began to get along sur-prisingly well. It turned out we had a lot in common after all and a great chemistry once things got rolling.

I soon discovered she was from Ottawa, and picked up her way of speak-ing while attending a private girl's boarding school in England during her formative years.

I finally gathered up the courage to ask her out on a date. I waited for a moment when we were alone on campus and said: "What say you and me get together some time for a drink or maybe dinner and a movie?"

Without pause she charmingly looked me in the eye, smiled brightly and said in a mien befitting her accent: "I would rather not, thank you."

I've had women get uncomfortable when I asked them out before and look away while replying with something like "sorry no," or give me fake phone numbers, or make a date and cancel at the last minute or even stand me up, but I'd never been shot down in such an elegant, classy manner before.

I just stood there unable to speak or even move. I had no idea how to respond. Finally she broke the silence.

"Very good. Move along now," she said as she subtly shooed me away with her hands. "There's a good lad!"

So I slowly backed away, wisely keeping my damn-fool mouth shut.

The next time we saw each other there was not a hint of awkwardness, as if she were used to being asked out all the time and had developed some kind of immunity. She did not treat me any differently and that made it less difficult. I was totally unprepared for what happened next.

Several weeks later Judy approached me in the cafeteria line and said: "So, when are we going for that drink and movie?"

I was flabbergasted.

What the hell happened? Suddenly she wants to go out with me? Should I ask her why she changed her mind? No! Better not look this gift horse in the mouth.

"How about tomorrow, then?" I said as smoothly as I could, which wasn't very.

"Okay, it's a date," Judy said with a cute grin as she handed me a piece of paper.

On it was her phone number and her name with an exclamation point and a little smiley face.

We went to see a Warren Beatty movie and had a drink afterwards. We kissed in my car outside her dorm. The date went well enough that we had another. And then another. Soon enough I met her Montreal friends. Judy and I even went to a karaoke bar one night and, hand in hand, sang the duet "Summer Nights" from *Grease* together.

Once word got out in the communications department that we were seeing each other, I became the target of resentment and scorn from all sides. It felt like all the boys were jealous and the girls started to dislike me because of my association with her.

Then something occurred that would prove to be an omen. Winter holiday break came along, and Judy went back to Ottawa for three weeks. She did not tell me when she was leaving, nor did she give me the means to contact her there, or even say goodbye or call to wish me a nice holiday season. She just left. I was confused and curious as to why she didn't at least give me a card or gift something, like I did but never got a chance to give her. After the holidays she returned and we picked up where we left off. I asked no questions. I was just relieved and grateful she'd come back to me.

Just about every week Judy took me with her friends to a bar on Bishop Street where Thursday was ladies' night. Women drank for free so the place was loaded with thirsty coeds and horny, misbehaving boys looking to score. When we hit the dance floor Judy would feel me up and kiss me more passionately than when we were in private, and certainly more than any other couple in the establishment.

Once during one of those evenings Judy's friend Cindy asked her if she could "borrow" me for a minute. Judy had no objection, and before I knew what was happening or had time to react or ask questions, Cindy grabbed my hand firmly and pulled me to the dance floor, where she aggressively held me tight, rubbed her body against mine, and gave me several deep, full-mouth kisses that confused the hell out of me. Of all of Judy's friends, she was the one I felt liked me the least; at times she was even a little contemptuous and hostile towards me.

Why is she doing this?

Meanwhile Judy sat at the bar watching us and not only did she not mind, but seemed oddly amused by it all.

Afterwards Judy explained that several young men were hassling Cindy on the dance floor, and she did that to ward them off. Would have been nice to at least tell me that beforehand; I would have cooperated. What was I going to do, give up a chance to kiss another beautiful woman, and with my girlfriend's blessing?

"Glad I could help," was the only thing I could think to say.

Smooth!

Some Thursdays I would pick Judy and her friends up and drive them to the bar; other times I would meet them at there. But always it would begin with an afternoon or early-evening phone call from Judy to set the time. On the first Thursday after the end of the winter semester, days before Judy was to go back to Ottawa for the summer, I didn't get a call. It was starting to get late; past the hour when we would usually arrive at the establishment. Mind you this was before the era of mobile communication, so I figured it was just an oversight, or I simply missed the call, and so I went anyway.

When they saw me arrive Judy's friends looked suspiciously over-amused. Judy blushed. I immediately knew it wasn't an oversight; they didn't want me there.

Judy quickly grabbed my hand and took me out on the dance floor. As she led me away I could hear one of her friends say: "I told you he'd show up!"

The next song was a slow dance and Judy wrapped her arms around my neck and pulled me in close for a deep kiss. Surprised I said: "Y'know Judy … I … I really like you … and mean I really like you a lot."

Judy looked up into my eyes and smiled uneasily.

"Maybe I should've told you what I'm like," she said as if guiltily confessing.

I stopped moving on the dance floor.

"I shouldn't have come tonight."

"I'm really sorry, Andreas," she said as her eyes began to turn red and swell like a dam about to burst.

"I'll go."

"I didn't mean for it to be like this."

"It's okay. I'm fine," I said, lying.

Wanting to leave before the awkwardness of the situation became a humiliation, I carefully backed away from her. After a few steps she turned around quickly, hiding her face as she rushed to the ladies' room.

Judy soon went back to Ottawa without calling, leaving me even more perplexed. I figured she had news for me; an explanation perhaps. I had no idea what she wanted from me or what we were all about.

And what exactly did she mean by "I should've told you what I'm like"?

I took it in stride, going so far as to date someone else during the summer. But when the new semester rolled around that relationship fizzled and I could not wait to see Judy again, optimistically and foolishly assuming we would be renewing our relationship like we did after the winter holiday.

When I saw her she was friendly but she seemed a little different; a little colder. We had lunch together on the first day of classes but she wouldn't hold my hand. After a few days I finally confronted her.

Judy told me she was involved with someone in Ottawa and was never looking for a steady relationship with me. Over the summer they had become serious and now we could no longer see each other.

It was quite a blow, but I took her explanation at face value and had the good sense for once not to make a fuss so we parted on good terms. By that time we had no classes together and I was spending more time with the down-to-earth students in the English Department, where I was minoring. I knew I would not run into her as often, and I didn't for the rest of the fall term. Or year for that matter. By the spring I had not seen her in so long I asked Phil, one of the few people in the communications department with whom I got along, and a friend of Judy's as well, if he had seen her. He informed me that she never returned from the latest winter holiday, and had dropped out of the university.

I thought I would never see or hear from her again.

Ten years later I found myself in Ottawa and decided to look her up. She was in the phone book so I dropped her a line. By her reaction I had the feeling she missed me like the world missed smallpox. We had a brief, clumsy, but friendly conversation and we did not end up seeing each other. Once again I felt like a clown.

About five years after that I was suddenly out of work and with plenty of time on my hands, so I joined a new internet social network that was gaining popularity and would soon engulf the planet. I first friended people I knew well, and eventually expanded to people with whom I had lost touch. Every time I made a new connection I would search their lists of friends for anyone I knew that I didn't find 100% objectionable, and a few I did. When I friended Phil, I scanned his list, and low and behold there was Judy. I took a chance and asked for her friendship (on the site at the time one could put what the past relationship was, and for her I put that we dated). A few days later she accepted my friendship and acknowledged that we had dated. But when I went over her list of friends, things suddenly started to make sense.

I was the only man she had dated. Judy had dated several other people, all women. And if that wasn't enough to give it away she had a recent picture of herself, a few pounds heavier, holding hands with a woman sporting a pair of round, metal-framed eyeglasses. And at the risk of sounding clichéd they could not have looked more like Peppermint Patty and Marcie from the old *Peanuts* comic strip if they had been drawn by Charles Schultz himself.

After a while I gathered up the courage to send her a message. We made on-line small talk and it was, well, it wasn't unpleasant at least. Finally I asked her why she went out with me in the first place.

I didn't intend on making her uncomfortable with that question, but I had to know and to her credit she answered me honestly.

Ever since she was quite young she'd known that she preferred female companionship. But it was a different time, and she was aware she would have to go to great lengths to hide her lifestyle. In England while at boarding school she had a secret girlfriend, but she outwardly dated a boy named Simon from the private boy's school that was paired with hers. Back home in Ottawa she had someone she cared about greatly, and there was another guy, a young man who lived in her neighbourhood whose parents, like hers and everybody else's in the nation's capital's endless suburbs, worked for the federal government, that she dated as a decoy. He was also for the longest time oblivious to her true self. In Montreal all the guys on campus where hitting on her, so she chose me as her shield.

"You know," I wrote, "my involvement with you made me a pariah at the Communications Department and prevented me from making friends."

She wrote back as only Judy could: "Don't be silly. You didn't lose anything. No one cared much for you anyway."

I have to say I still admire her directness.

"Of all the guys at school why did you chose me?" I asked.

Was it because she liked me? Because I was so handsome? Smart? Interesting? Cool? Because she thought I was a great guy?

Of course not.

The reason she selected me for the honour was because most of the students at the university were for some reason afraid of me and she figured if we were dating, they would leave her alone. Judy's logic was sound because it worked. Same deal with ladies night. The first time she went with her friends they were groped and manhandled on the dance floor by a bunch of inebriated jerks. She brought me along so they would leave her alone and they could get loaded on the free booze, and only one jerk, although a sober one, would grope and manhandle them. And I could drive them home safely, to boot.

I should have been angrier, after all I really liked her and spent a long time wondering why it didn't work with us; at times it tormented me. And I hate dishonesty. But I also understood how difficult it would have been for her back then to live freely. This was before Ellen DeGeneres came out and that lifestyle, while then making steady progress, was still far from gaining mainstream acceptance. Then Judy told me she was committed to her partner and now lives her life openly. There were some rough times, but her parents and family have accepted them and she is now comfortable with her life and how she was living it, and I am glad she is happy.

That was the last time I contacted her. A few years later, I'm not sure when or for what reason, Judy quietly "unfriended" me.

BURNED BIKERS

When my brother turned eighteen he went for his motorcycle license. While still taking the course he brought home a copy of *Cycle World* magazine to look at various makes and models, eventually settling on the Honda Nighthawk. (He was enough of a pragmatist to understand that Harleys were way out of his reach.)

Already into rock and roll, it was easy for me to take an interest in motorcycles as well. I started reading the articles and looking at the photographs of rugged, leather-clad outlaws riding free. I saved up and bought my own cool leather motorcycle jacket. I had it all figured out: First I'd get my regular driver's licence, then when I was eighteen I'd get my motorcycle permit, just like Peter. After a few years of saving I'd be tooling around on my very own Harley-Davidson, if only to one-up him. Yes, I dared to dream.

When I told my father about my plans he waved his hands and said: "Ahh! No! Forget about *eet*. People have too many accidents with the motorcycle!"

"But what about Peter?" I asked.

"Peter, he *eez* good driver. You, you would have accident. And beside, you are not a motorcycle person. *Eet eez* not for you!"

Not for me? I'll be the judge of that, thank you!

A few months after that I found myself perusing the motorcycle section of the Multimags store on Ste. Catherine Street and had an experience that I will never forget: I was checking out a copy of *Biker's Lifestyle*, when I turned and saw a huge man standing next to me – at least 6-foot-5, and wearing a leather motorcycle vest with an eagle and the Harley-Davidson logo on the back. He had long black hair on the left side of his head. When he turned in my direction I first noticed he didn't have any hair on the right side, because he had suffered severe burns. In place of his right arm was a stump that was covered in melted tattoos. His right ear was missing, and he walked with a decided limp. He was leafing through a copy of a motorcycle magazine with his remaining hand.

I was completely caught off guard by his appearance; so shocked I stared like a fool for what was certainly too long and could feel myself starting to sweat. Fortunately the lumbering giant paid no attention to me. Right then and there I put away my copy of *Biker's Lifestyle*, and picked up a copy of *Car and Driver*. And I never considered getting a motorcycle again.

In the late '90's I had a girlfriend named Melanie who lived on the top floor of a triplex in Ville Emard. One Friday evening I arrived at her place after work and she was very excited. Some new neighbours had just moved into the basement apartment.

She was enthusiastic about this because her building was a bit of a seedy tenement and most of the other renters were not in her age group or were difficult and unfriendly. The new people were a young couple like us and she said they seemed nice. She told me the girl was called Julie, and her boyfriend was a tattoo artist named Jean-Marc; Mel was anxious for me to meet them.

"I know you will like them, *eh*. They 'ave a dog just like you and they are really cool," she said.

"Also just like me!" I said.

Mel rolled her eyes and said: "Yeah, sure."

I was up or it, and soon enough we were knocking on their door. The front entrance to the apartment opened into a narrow hallway. Julie was on one side, while Jean-Marc was hidden behind the door. Julie was a very attractive, petite blonde. After Mel and I entered, Julie closed the front door to reveal her boyfriend.

His face had suffered burns, similar to those of the Multimags behemoth; only his entire face was scarred and he had no eyebrows. About two-thirds of his scalp was covered with short curly, blonde, almost white, locks of hair not unlike that of a young lamb. The left side had none, and his left ear was just a nub. I was startled and unprepared and he could tell. Everyone could tell.

After exchanging pleasantries Julie, Mel and I went to their living room while Jean-Marc went to the kitchen to get back to a phone call we had interrupted with our arrival. Their dog was a beautiful golden retriever.

"Andréas, là," Mel said, *"il a une chienne aussi, là. Elle s'appelle Isabella, là."*

"Isabella, là?" She says "là" even when the last word ends in a "là" already? Isn't there a set of rules for that? What does she call Los Angeles? La-La-Land, là?

I felt like a total heel and when Jean-Marc got off the phone, I sought him out to apologize for my reaction. We shared a smoke in the kitchen, and he was incredibly cool about the whole thing, saying that he was used to it and understanding enough to know that if the situation were reversed, he would probably do the same thing.

"May I ask how it happened? Was it a motorcycle accident?"

"Oui," he said and he proceeded to recount the story to me: A few years earlier he was racing down a stretch of highway at night with a friend. They were both on Japanese speed bikes, which he referred to as a "couple of rice rockets." They were attempting to see if they could top 200 kilometers per hour.

200 kilometres an hour? I don't event feel comfortable doing that in an airplane!

As he continued to explain in a highly animated fashion, he was going faster than he ever had before when his ride started to wildly oscillate in what he referred to as either a "tank-slapper" or a "death wobble" at various points in the story. Before he knew it he was skidding and eventually crashed. His fuel tank ruptured, spraying gasoline all over his face and torso. A spark from his motor ignited a horrible fireball.

"I was very lucky, especially because I was not wearing an *'elmet.* I could *'ave* injured my spine or lost an arm or leg or worse: My *'ands,* and then my job, *eh*? Bye-bye! I was wearing leather gloves *t'ey* protected me, *eh*, so I could at least still work. Instead all I *'ad* were burns. I *breat'ed* also a little fire, so I got a little burned inside, *eh*." He took another drag from his cigarette, determined to finish the job on his lungs. "But like I say I am lucky. *Everyt'ing* still work," he said with a nudge and a wink that would put Eric Idle to shame.

So I related to him my story about wanting a motorcycle and the guy at the Multimags and how that turned me off to the idea.

"Ah-Ah-Ah!" Jean-Marc said, laughing. "What are you, a baby? You get scare so easy? I tell you what, when I get out of the *'ospital,* I right away get back on another bike, my friend let me use *'is ...*"

What a great friend! Nice enough to lend him a bike to complete the run that failed to kill him the first time. And his friend had no fear that Jean-Marc would wreck this cycle as well?

"… and go on the same *'ighway*, again *wit'* no *'elmet*, and this time I make two *'undred* kilometer! Easy!"

He what!?! Does he not realize how fortunate he was the first time? Why would he chance something like that again? What is wrong with this guy? He won't be happy until he becomes a headless torso!?! How bad does the accident have to be!?!

We stayed for another hour before they had to go out and meet some friends for a late dinner. After Mel and I returned to her place I asked her why she wasn't so shocked upon seeing Jean-Marc.

"Oh," she replied, "I *'ad* seen *'im* when I met *'dem* in the afternoon."

"What!?!" I shouted. "You knew? Why the hell didn't you warn me?"

"I forgot."

"How could you forget something like that? I made a fool of myself in front of the guy. I mean, he was cool about it, but what if he wasn't? It's not some minor detail, or something!"

"Okay, I'm sorry. Gee! Stop being such a baby!"

In my adult life I had never before been called a baby twice by two different people on the same day.

About three weeks later Melanie and I broke up. It had nothing to do with that incident, though. And I never saw the couple again.

To this day I wonder if I ever really had the nerve to be a true biker. Here were two guys who despite horrific accidents were still into it, and I'm giving up just because of something that happened to people I didn't even know that well.

I guess Dad knew what he was talking about the whole time.

A SOUVENIR OF LETTERMAN

Anyone who grew up in Park Ex in the '70's and '80's lived in the shadow of the CFCF-12 television station building at 405 Ogilvy Avenue. Besides hockey Hall-of-Famer Dickie Moore and Hollywood actor Glenn Ford, it was the most famous thing about our neighbourhood.

An English-language television station, CFCF is seen throughout Quebec. When I was young they showed *The Flintstones* from 12 to 12:30 p.m., and *The Price is Right* from 5 to 6 p.m. Then there was *Pulse News*.

From time to time we would see some of the on-air personalities in the restaurants and stores around Park Ex; it was something to brag about in the schoolyard. At least once a month my father would come home from work and say he had the weatherman or sportscaster or one of the reporters as a fare in his cab. That place was part of the landscape. Something we took pride in, like a home team.

When I registered at Dawson College I was finally allowed to take any courses I wanted, so I went into the Creative Arts program and studied film and broadcasting, as well as music and just about whatever caught my interest. While there I found I had a knack for this kind of thing and decided that maybe I should try to get a job at CFCF after graduation. And as a bonus I could walk to work every day! After two and a half years I got my DEC and discovered I had some real talent, so I decided to reach even higher. I mean, why be limited to Park Ex, when there was a whole world out there?

During my college years the greatest 1-2-3 combination in the history of late night TV was on NBC: It was Carson at 11:30, Letterman at 12:30, and *Later with Bob Costas* closing it off at 1:30. Nothing on the tube in that era, not even on primetime, was as entertaining.

I decided to try and get a job, any job, on *Late Night with David Letterman*. I put together a fifteen minute demo tape of some of the productions I was involved in at Dawson and sent it to Steve O'Donnell, the Head Writer on *Late Night*, and started from there. I FedExed it and a copy of my CV to his office at Rockefeller Plaza, and started calling him to make sure he received it. After a few failed attempts, he eventually took my call. I was so surprised I hardly knew what to say at first, but he was friendly, approachable and pleasant, and after an awkward start things settled down and we talked about the TV business for a few minutes. He told me he received the package I sent him, remembering it because of my unique name, and agreed to watch my tape. He also said he liked my Canadian accent.

Always one to push my luck, I decided to try Toronto. I was still in touch with an old high school teacher named Mrs. Sheehy, whose sister-in-law happened to be the producer of a televised morning news program that was broadcast nationally. Mrs. Sheehy was nice enough to put us together and The Producer agreed to meet with me if I ever came to the big town. I did some more research and made more calls to a number of TV and radio stations in the GTA and the following summer I headed down the 401 in a bus with a bag full of tapes and CV's ready to take on the Queen City.

I was lucky enough to score a free place to stay: Some friends of Mom's who lived in The Danforth had an extra room, so I was set. My first day I started making calls, and eventually I got through to The Producer again. We discussed a good time to meet.

"Well," she said, "we are really busy right now. We are getting ready to go to Tokyo for the announcement of who will get the 1996 summer games. And I am having lunch with our new host, R.B. Richards at noon."

R.B. Richards was a former V.J. from a national music cable channel who was making the great leap from interviewing Wendy O. Williams to world leaders. He eventually became a White House correspondent for an American television network.

She finally told me she could give me thirty minutes of her time at 11 a.m., for which I was infinitely grateful. I showed up a half hour early and waited in the outer office. Everyone there was really nice to me. The outgoing host, a 35-year veteran of the TV news game, was sitting at his desk nearby talking on the phone.

Right on time The Producer summoned me to her windowed office, and we sat and had a pleasant chat about careers in broadcasting. As promised the meeting ended at exactly 11:30 and she agreed to see my tape and look at my CV. She even gave me one of the show's signature coffee mugs, usually reserved just for staff and guests who appear on air. I thanked her profusely and left. (I still have the mug in question.)

The elevator was closing when I heard: "Wait, hold the door!" I quickly hit the "open" button and none other than The Host boarded.

"Lobby, please," he said but I had already pushed that. "How do you know (The Producer)?" The Host asked.

"Oh, she's a friend of a friend. I just finished school and I'm looking for work in broadcasting."

"Well, good luck," he said.

After a few awkward seconds, I said: "So, I hear you're leaving?"

"What!?!" he immediately shot back with a confused and angry look.

Holy shit! He doesn't know? What the hell? Why would she so casually tell me, some schmuck off the street, if it was such a secret!?! I didn't ask her! I didn't prod her! Why didn't she tell me not to tell anyone? What the fuck kind of place is this? And here I am, some fucking idiot stranger, telling this guy his career is over!

I had to think fast.

"You're leaving ... the building now? I've ... I've never been here before. How do I get out?"

Just then the elevator doors opened to the lobby, and not thirty feet away were the unmistakable large glass front doors.

"They're right there," he said, pointing.

"Oh, yes. Of course. Thank you. It was nice meeting you," I said as I slowly backed away from him. "Really very nice to meet you. I'm a big fan. Love your show. Ah, have a good day!"

I walked through the front doors as fast as I could without looking like I was in a hurry. Once I got outside and down the front steps, I wasn't sure what to do next. So I pivoted and ran as fast as I could down the street in the blistering summer sun. I got about two blocks before I ran out of breath. I stopped, saturated with my own perspiration, and leaned onto a lamppost repeating "Omigod, omigod, omigod," while panting like an El Paso Rottweiler guarding a trailer park meth lab.

Despite meeting several people, including the then head of CBC sitcom development, the trip yielded nothing. I didn't hear back from the morning show, and I was too embarrassed to ever call there again. I'm still surprised they didn't hire an assassin to hunt me down. So I decided to continue my academic career, eventually enrolling in Concordia University's Communications program.

I continued to call O'Donnell several times a year; sometimes he took the call and we'd talk for a few minutes. But I was sure he never saw my tape, or if he did he either didn't like it, or forgot about it, which I guess is the same thing.

During that time Letterman went from NBC to CBS. I kept calling.

After graduation I went to New Jersey on a car trip vacation with The Weasel and his girlfriend. We stopped in New York City on the way and I dragged them to the side door of the Ed Sullivan theatre to see if we could catch David Letterman arriving for work. We weren't there for five minutes when who should show up but the tall, blonde, bespectacled mid-westerner Steve O'Donnell.

I approached him and introduced myself. He was polite, but had no recollection of our conversations. I told him I just received my degree in communications and asked about career opportunities.

"Good to see you graduated," he said, "but there is very little I can do to hire you. You would have to be the child of a CBS executive or something just to get an internship."

"Okay, but can you at least get me tickets for the show tonight?" hoping I could finagle him into at least inviting us in to see the studio or maybe their offices.

"Can't even do that I'm afraid," he said. He then told me how I could write for tickets.

We talked for a few more minutes and then he said he had to go. We shook hands and that was it. Soon afterwards he left the show to write for *The Simpsons* and *Seinfeld*.

The Weasel and his girlfriend just stared at us the whole time probably thinking: "Who the fuck is this guy and how does Andre know him?"

We ended up taking the NBC tour later that day, which was fun. We saw John Chancellor in the lobby. He was quite small. And fellow Canadian Keith Morrison. He was rather tall.

When I got home I wasted no time sending in a postcard for show tickets. About six to eight weeks later I received a postcard with a black and white image of Dave waving and smiling sarcastically. The back of the postcard said that because of incredible demand, tickets to the show were given away lottery style. If I don't hear anything within six months, I should try again.

I put the postcard in a safe place and waited. And waited. By Christmas I had given up hope of ever getting tickets; dozens of times I had sent away for passes to *Saturday Night Live*, and to this day I have still not heard back. Someone told me once that even if you were granted tickets to *SNL*, you were not likely to get in. They overbook, and on top of that most seats are reserved for friends of the cast, crew, host and guest band, and I couldn't afford to go all the way to New York City on a maybe.

On January the 10th 1995, almost exactly at the six-month mark, there came a letter from CBS. Inside were two tickets to the Tuesday January the 17th, 1995 taping of *The Late Show with David Letterman*! I hit the roof. Then I realized I had less than a week to make the necessary arrangements, so I leapt into action.

My bosses at the record store where I worked were cool and rearranged my schedule to give me the following Monday, Tuesday, and Wednesday off. I'd lose a day's pay, and have to work nine days in a row the week after, but that was okay with me. One of them went so far as to mock me for expending so much effort and money just to attend the taping of a one-hour show with tickets that, like *SNL*, don't even guarantee admission.

"What? This from the guy who once hitch-hiked to Syracuse for a Grateful Dead concert, after having already seen The Dead over fifty times," I said.

That shut him up.

My next step was getting there and finding an affordable place to crash. For that I called the CAA's travel agency. They booked passage for me on an overnight train to the Big Apple, and found me a room at a Midtown Manhattan motor lodge that was a bargain because it was off-season and the motel was undergoing renovations.

Step 3: The Weasel agreed to give me a ride to and from Montreal's Central Station.

Now, what to do with the extra ticket? I had no girlfriend at the time. Not even any prospects. Peter couldn't change his work schedule and none of my friends were big enough Letterman fans to change their workdays around and pay for the trip, especially on such short notice. (I later found out The Weasel would have gone, but it never even occurred to me to ask him because he always thought that Letterman was lame, and I didn't think he could get off work so easily. I'm still not sure why my best friend, who is always so driven and aggressive in career and with his personal life, suddenly became too shy to tell me he'd like to go.) So I decided to go solo and see if I could sell the extra ticket or give it away to someone in New York.

I was hitched-up and ready to ride.

While waiting in line at Central Station, I met a pretty, young American college student named Regina. We seemed to hit it off right away, and as it turned out, we were on the same train. She was going home to Philadelphia after a long weekend partying with some friends in Montreal, and immediately zoomed to the top of the extra ticket list.

Because our final destinations were different, we were assigned places in separate cars, but the moment we started to move I paid her a visit. We chatted away until reaching the border and I was forced to return to my assigned seat in order to pass customs.

After we got rolling again I wasted no time returning to her. No sooner did I sit down than she asked me to buy her a beer; she said she was twenty, and a person had to be at least twenty-one to buy booze in New York State. It's illegal to buy alcohol for minors, so I of course went straight to the dining car and bought a couple of Budweiser's. I was in New York for less than ten minutes, and already I was committing crimes.

"Here," I said, "this Bud's for you!"

"What!?!" she said, not getting the reference. The brewery paid millions to advertise their slogan for nothing, it seems.

"Forget it," I said.

Within minutes we made the first of what would be many stops to take on more passengers. I had to get back to my seat to avoid losing my space to someone who thought it unoccupied. By the time we were back on our way I returned to Regina, only to find both beer cans empty and her fast asleep. (Or maybe pretending to be so to avoid further contact with me, I don't know.) She stayed that way the rest of the voyage, and I never got to talk to her again let alone offer up the extra ticket.

At one point during the trip I woke up at 4 a.m. to find the train stopped at a rural, jerkwater station. I stepped out on the platform to have a smoke and stretch my legs. The place was dark and there wasn't another soul in sight. While exploring I suddenly realized: *What if they take off without me? I'd be trapped!* I rushed back and not ten seconds after boarding, the doors closed without any warning and the train slowly departed the lonely depot.

We arrived in New York on time to an unseasonably mild morning; the temperature got to about 12 degrees Celsius that day. The motel was decent and as advertised, under renovation. I caught forty winks, showered, and made it to the Ed Sullivan Theatre by noon. A helpful CBS page numbered my tickets and I had time to grab some lunch and the cooperative weather allowed me to take a stroll through Central Park.

The show featured star of *The X-Files* David Duchovny, actor Laurence Fishburne, and singer Tom Jones. I got a seat in the second row, on the right. The theatre was, as advertised, colder than a meat locker. The atmosphere, however, was warm, loose and fun, similar to that of a rock concert. (Just a few days before going Dave said on the air that in order to truly enjoy the show, one would have to come to the theatre. And he was right.)

The band came out a preformed two songs, followed by Dave himself as he gave away a large canned ham. Then the real show began.

Dave's opening skit was making fun of strange, real products found at the local grocery store. One of them was a 6-foot long piece of beef jerky. After the first commercial, Dave went into the audience, tore the giant jerky up, and handed it out. I was briefly shown on camera eating the piece he gave me.

After the extravaganza, the audience exited from the theatre's side doors. Some people hurried to see Laurence Fishburne as he made a B-line to his limousine.

I waited by the side office tower entrance. I had an extra, unused ticket, and I was determined to have Dave autograph it.

I waited for several hours with someone who looked like he worked on Wall Street, and a trio of women from Nebraska. The weather turned cold, windy and unfriendly since the sun set, and I was starting to get a monster headache. Finally, pay dirt!

First came his long-time assistant Laurie Diamond. She was polite, friendly and all smiles, almost as if she were making up for Dave being so cold, gruff and curt. She apologized in advance saying that Dave was tired and on his way to tape a future segment for the show, so he may seem a tad unpleasant.

Dave emerged. I had neglected to bring my camera, so the ticket was all I had. He let his picture be taken with the Nebraska women.

I held out my hand and said: "Thanks for the beef jerky!" like a total moron. It was all I could think to say.

Dave shot me a confused look as though he had no idea what I was talking about. *Had Dave already forgotten what he did on his own show?* I had no chance to explain. Dave took my hand and shook it firmly while mumbling something I didn't quite get, but I was too nervous to ask him to repeat himself.

Just before climbing into his limo, he grabbed the pen and the extra ticket I had outstretched and signed it. A moment later the car pulled away, and it was over. I stood alone on a dark, quiet New York side street.

I had supper at Planet Hollywood, took a walk through Times Square, and went back to my motel. I had to catch a 7 a.m. train the next day.

It was then I noticed that not only was my motel under severe renovation, but that my entire floor except for my room was blocked off with no lighting outside my door. In fact, my whole time there I didn't see another guest. If some lunatic were to break into my room, which was easily accessible, no one would hear my screams just before being bludgeoned to death. I pushed a chair and some other furniture against my door.

What if the maniac burst through the window? Oh well …

That evening I watched my appearance on the *Late Show with David Letterman*. I had always dreamed of being a guest on his show, and that became the closest I will ever come.

I got up at 5 a.m., had breakfast at a local diner, and caught my train. The ride back was amazing: A sunny day through the Adirondacks with melting snow creating spectacular waterfalls along the cliffs that lined the tracks. I pressed the side of my head to the window and watched the natural show as it raced by.

The Weasel picked me up on time (for once) at the station, and the first words out of his mouth were: "How was the beef jerky?"

The Weasel, who had never watched *Letterman* in his life, had seen the show. Not only that, but he went out on his balcony and called Sam and his crew, who were gathered outside, over to watch. They freaked out when they saw me.

"How did you know I would get on camera?" I asked.

"I know you. When you are determined, you find a way."

I still have the tape of that show. I lost it for a while, but rediscovered it recently while cleaning out a cabinet. I still look at it from time to time. There's me, in my mid-twenties, with a mullet and wearing a cheesy, old leather motorcycle jacket, eating beef jerky on TV. And for the briefest of moments, I was the only thing on CBS, to paraphrase Dave.

The jerky may be gone, but I mounted the postcard, as well as the used and unused autographed tickets on a picture frame. To this day it still hangs in my bedroom and remains one of my prized possessions, a souvenir of time I met David Letterman.

THE RED VELOUR ROPES

It was always difficult for me to make friends around the neighbourhood. I usually made connections at school, but as soon as the summer came around I didn't get to see them every day because most kids in Park Ex spent their entire summers in Greece, or hung out with their cousins.

My brother was not the typical mean and bullying first-born and let me hang with him and his friends. In Park Ex because all the Greek kids had the same names (George, Nick, John, Chris, etc. ...) we usually called each other by our last names, with the exception of George T., whose surname was so long it spanned two time zones. His group already had a "Peter" so my brother was called "Kessaris" and despite there not being another Andreas they referred me "Kessaris, Jr." to which I would object with: "I'm his brother, not his son!" Like most Greeks named Andreas in Quebec, I am often called Andre. There are numerous parallel English versions of Greek names that are often employed in an attempt to Canadianize them. For example, Fotis becomes Frank. Despina becomes Debbie. Vassilios is Bill or Billy. Yiannis is John. Eleni is Helen. Demitrios becomes Jimmy. In fact my brother's birth name is actually Panagiotis. Kostas in Toronto or Chicago is somehow Gus, but for reasons I remain unsure of they don't do that in Montreal.

Still they treated me well and when I was unable to keep up with them they showed me mercy and waited. Many of my older cousins horribly abused their younger siblings. One afternoon during Christmas vacation I went to a cousin's house a few blocks over. We were both in elementary school at the time and planned to go see a movie together. After leaving his house we rounded a corner and happened upon his eldest brother and the gang of Sir William Hingston Comprehensive High School-trained toughs he led around the neighbourhood. (Hingston High, named after a former Mayor of Montreal, was Park Ex's only secondary school, and had a reputation of being a lawless breeding ground for thugs and future criminals; the provincial penitentiary was considered by many a safer place. It was part of the Catholic School Commission, so most students who went to Barclay did not go there afterwards because it would require registration in a completely new school board; and besides most Greeks did not want their kids at a Catholic school. I never quite understood why.)

"Get him!" his older brother yelled.

"Run!" my peer cried, and we were off, but they were all high-school aged and quickly cornered us in a snowy alley. They grabbed us both but then I heard my older cousin say: "No! Not him!" and they released me. He was astute and feared I would squeal on him … and he was correct. If they harmed me I would have ran straight to my mom and sung like Pavarotti (which was likely the reason why that gang never hassled me), and my mom would've told their mom; no matter how mean or bold they appear be, every Greek fears his mother. My aunt had a broken half a hockey stick she used to discipline her children. I never actually saw her hit them with it, but witnessed her wield it menacingly on multiple occasions.

He had them take his younger brother and rub his face in the snow (yellow snow, no less), then they pantsed him; he was left lying face-down in the snow crying as they walked away high-fiving each other.

I stood over him and was so shocked that I couldn't think of a thing to say. Finally I asked: "Do you still want to go to the movies?" He didn't answer. So I went home.

When I returned my mother asked why I was back so soon, and I told her what happened.

"They didn't touch you, did they?" she asked.

"Nah, they left me alone," I answered.

"Oh, okay," she said.

So it could have been way worse for me. I was lucky my brother and his friends weren't like that.

During the summers boys often organized informal street hockey games in the seemingly endless schoolyards as well as the ubiquitous alleyways and lanes that crisscrossed Park Ex. I was never an outstanding athlete. In fact, in high school I was the gym class joke, but when I was eight I figured if I got a hockey stick I could join in the games and make some friends of my own. Cheap street hockey sticks at the time were sold at the local *dépanneurs* and cost about $8 each. They were made by name manufacturers but were low end and the blades had no curve; not something one would use for a league game, but they were good enough for the street. The *dep* also sold plastic replacement blades that could be attached to the end of a damaged stick with screws when its original blade cracked or shattered, which was often given their poor quality.

I asked my dad for the money and his reply was: "Ahh, what do you want that for!?!" Figuring I would have to do this myself, I began to save my money. That's not true. In reality, I felt it was easier to do an end run around my dad and asked my mom, who gave me the $8 when I explained it would help me make friends and get me out of the house.

It wasn't long before I saw a game being played in the schoolyard at Barclay. I ran home and grabbed my new Sherwood and immediately returned. I didn't know most of the boys playing, but some of them were kids I saw around school. When I asked if I could play too they looked at each other and declared that their game was finished and took their nets and left. I went home, put my stick back into the hall storage closet, and decided to go bike riding instead. After tooling around the neighbourhood for a while I came across the same boys playing in a nearby lane. They moved their game just to avoid playing with me.

The hockey stick remained forgotten until I was nineteen and we moved from the Stuart Avenue address. I discovered it at the back of the closet while cleaning it out. It was so small I couldn't believe that it was ever for me. Unused and covered in dust, I decided to leave it behind. Maybe the new tenants would have better luck with it.

* * *

My first full-time payroll job out of university was in a record store in a small shopping mall located in an upper-middle class suburb far and away from Park Ex. One day a new hire who lived in that area named Hill started working with me. She was nineteen, and just slightly over five feet tall with long, thick brown curly hair. Hill was starting Concordia University's Communications program, from which I had graduated several years earlier.

We also both had a desire to become writers. We became fast friends, and for three years a week didn't go by where Hill and I didn't hang out. Mostly we went to my favourite café called *Le Figaro*, an amazing anachronistic place nestled on the corner of Fairmount and Hutchison in Outremont – during Montreal's all-too-brief summer they open an outdoor terrace that reminded one of my exes of Van Gogh's *Café de nuit*; every time I'm there I feel like I'm in Paris ... I hope that place never changes – and we'd talk about TV, music, movies and writing.

She was unique and quirky; once playing Shania Twain's "Honey I'm Home" on a continuous loop in the store until the manager had had enough. Hill was flighty and spoke quickly, often saying things like: "Oh my god that is, like, soooo not funny! Like, totally!" (That was after I had made a joke at her expense about her lack of height.) The first time I visited her at her parents' Hampstead mansion, I noticed she had a spacious, elaborate bedroom with large, wooden blue and white cabinets that were obviously custom designed for her when she was young. Hill had a painting canvas on an easel and was in the process of copying a photo from a magazine. When I went by again few weeks later all the cabinets were ripped out. The room was bare, not even a poster. The only furniture was a queen-sized bed and a new computer desk with her Mac. She told me she was going to completely re-do the room. The painting remained about 10% done on the easel. In subsequent trips to her home work on the painting had not advanced. It was never completed, and eventually she tossed it. And I never saw any new furniture.

In what was to be one of numerous long conversations at *Le Figaro* she was telling me about her new courses at Concordia.

"This one communications class, it's like, totally the bomb!"

"Oh, I'm sorry. Do you plan to drop it?"

"No, Andreas," she replied, "'the bomb' is a good thing."

There I was in my mid-twenties and already I was talking like someone's unhip parent.

One day Hill called me up and said that there was a "totally cool" bar on Ontario Street East that we should check out. It was a trendy new place that played big band style music, which in the mid-90's enjoyed a short-lived revival, and they served dozens of different kinds of martinis, some clear, some green and some the colour of Windex.

"And," she said, "last week Jim Carey and Nicholas Cage were so there! Isn't that, like, totally awesome? Omigod!" (Nic Cage was in Montreal at the time filming a movie called *Snake Eyes*. Stories of his sightings were common at the time like Bigfoot in the Pacific Northwest. In what was yet another odd coincidence for me, a few years later I dated someone whose cousin, a graphic designer well-connected in the movie business, was the one who brought the Hollywood stars there.)

"That sounds a little exclusive," I said. "Do you think they would let us in?"

"Oh, for sure! The coat-check boy is, like, a friend of mine. We can totally get in. C'mon, let's go."

Against my better judgement we went that night. On the way there Hill confessed that she really didn't care about the club; she wanted to go because she had a thing for the aforementioned coat-check attendant, who was a classmate of hers at Concordia. When we arrived there was a line-up outside being controlled by stanchions with red velour ropes. I didn't care for the way they were herded in the cold like cattle and wanted to leave, but Hill insisted that she could get us in. She approached the doorman and told him that she was friends with one of the employees. They went inside to see and while I waited outside at the front door a group approached me.

"Excuse me sir," one of them said, "we were here before, so do we have to wait in line again?"

He thought I was doorman. Smartly resisting the temptation to say "sure, go right in!" I instead told them the truth. Hill and the doorman came out soon after.

"We're cool!" she proudly declared.

The place was nothing special. The multi-hued martinis tasted like, well, like martinis. The atmosphere was superficial and most of the people there were pretentious, shallow, artsy young hipsters and trendies; not the kind of place either of us enjoyed. And it wasn't over-crowded; it could have easily accommodated the people waiting outside. I realized then that they were being played. The Bouncer had no intention of granting them admission. They were herded there in the hopes they would give up and leave, because they were not the *right* people. Still, we went back several times to the point where the doorman recognized us and automatically allowed entry. We were finally, like the song goes, "in with the in crowd."

Around that time Hill and I chose a cold and wet weeknight to go for a coffee at her favourite café on Monkland Avenue. We met a waitress there named Betsy, who seemed nice. She was tall and slender, with pixie hair dyed burgundy. We began a conversation. She was a jazz dancer from London England who was in town for a year. And she was impressed that we worked at a record shop, although I never told her it was a lame chain store in an even lamer suburban mall. Hill rolled her eyes as I asked Betsy what time she finished work and if she wanted to go out afterwards. She said yes.

"She is, like, so totally going to stand you up, Andreas," Hill said as I drove her home. "Don't, like, even bother going back."

"I have nothing to lose by going back," I said.

"Omigod, you are, like, so gullible. How about your dignity? How about that?"

Ha! When it comes to losing dignity, she didn't know who she was dealing with!

Betsy was in fact there waiting for me at closing time and I took her to a Bishop Street pub (the same one I went to with Judy) for drinks. The bar was relatively empty but it was a completely wrong place for a sophisticated bohemian like Betsy. In hindsight I should have taken her to a more avant-garde establishment along the Main. We talked about music, and like most Brits she was extremely knowledgeable. Half the time I just nodded like I knew what she was talking about when in fact I had no clue. At least I was able to fake may way through.

"Do you like Gerry & the Gerkhovz?" she asked.

"Yeah, they're great."

"What was your favourite album?"

"Oh, their first, of course!"

"Of course, the first is always the best; with the most integrity."

I drove her to where she was residing, the 3rd floor of a huge industrial loft on De la Gauchetiére, a lifestyle likely inspired by Andy Warhol's The Factory. She was staying there with innumerable artists and craftspeople, including some members of a hot local indie punk band called Scotty & the Wangkerz. Although she seemed less than impressed with me, I was able to procure her phone number.

I managed to finagle a second date about a week later that went a little better, at least at first.

After dinner in Chinatown we walked back to the loft. We stood in the arched doorway of her building to avoid the drizzle that persisted that night, awkwardly chatting. I slowly, slightly leaned my head forward to give her a kiss. She adroitly moved her head to the right and said: "Would you like to come upstairs and meet everyone? The band is being featured on a radio station tonight and we are having a listening party."

"I'm game," I said.

"You're *whaaat?*" she said in a way only an English accent could.

"I said 'I'm *game*,'" I said again.

"Oh," she said, "I thought you said 'I'm *gay.*'"

Really? I just tried to kiss her. Why would she think I said that?

A local commercial radio station had a weekly program called *Made in Canada* which featured an hour-long profile of a Canadian band. This week it was Scotty & the Wangkerz's turn.

Betsy brought me in and introduced me around, but everyone looked at me and my square, out-of-date rocker clothing and more or less blew me off as though my very existence offended them. Betsy did not object to any of that. Despite working at a record store for starvation wages, the fact that I possessed a motorized vehicle, albeit an old beater, made me bourgeois, even though I'm sure more than a few of those jokers were living off trust funds and savings bonds their parents and grandparents accumulated for them so they could laze around all day, take drugs, and act superior to people who actually worked for a living.

It was at that point that I realized she probably saw me again just for the free meal. Before the show was on I sat at a table where the leader of the band and someone else were engaged in a conversation about how lawyers in the U.S. were money-grubbing scum that were clogging the court system (I later found out that one of them was in law school), something that apparently wasn't happening in Canada because we had no fault insurance.

"Well," I said, "as flawed a system as they have, it's still better than having people settle things in the street with firearms, which are ridiculously easy to get down there."

I mistakenly thought that they would appreciate my logic and opinion, but instead their delicate egos did not like being shown-up, making me further an outcast. They would not even acknowledge that I had made a valid point. They simple paused for a moment, and continued as if I had said nothing. Scotty & the Wangkerz's popularity was gaining momentum, and they were about to be the subject of a big-time radio show, so their leader had to be nothing less than an infallible god. Who the hell was I to have an opinion?

The broadcast began and during the first commercial break, one of the band members loudly and hatefully slammed the show's host, a multi-decade veteran and local radio legend who has since been inducted into the Canadian Radio Broadcasters' Hall of Fame.

"He was wearing old 70's-style rocker clothes," he said in what may also have been a pointed jab at me. "He asked a question from his notes, and as we were answering it he didn't pay attention to what we were saying! He just looked down at the next question on his list!"

"Look," I said, "I have a BA in communications from Concordia and studied journalism as well at Dawson; that is how we are taught to do interviews. Why are you complaining anyway? This could only help your band. He didn't have to put you on the air. You weren't doing him any favours. There are literally a hundred bands out there who would kill for that same exposure you're getting for free."

I should have added "you ungrateful scumbag!" to that because the die was cast and they were never going to respect me anyway. If there was anyone left in the room that did not already despise me, they certainly did by now. I even heard a faint "who invited him?" in the background. The show was back from commercial and they all quickly huddled around the radio again. I took that as my cue, and slipped out unnoticed without saying bye to anyone.

I called Betsy several days later and while she politely took the call, she was in no mood to converse with me. But I still had an ace in the hole: I could get her into the trendy bar.

Date #3!

I picked her up on a Saturday night and we went straight to the bar. I knew I was taking a chance the same doorman would be there; a gamble that paid off. We were soon inside and I was scoring points. At least I thought I was. After about an hour, Betsy turned to me and said that she had had enough of the place and knew of a cool party that was going on at a university professor's place nearby on St. Denis Street.

We were soon at the party and I immediately noticed a game of Trivial Pursuit about to start in the living room. Betsy began talking with some people she knew and when she saw how much I wanted to play she insisted that I partake. So I partook. I was soon leading the game when I asked someone if they had seen her.

"The girl you came with? Really pale? Pixie hair? She left about half an hour ago with some girls," someone said.

"Oh man, brutal," one of the other Trivial Pursuit players said. "Dude, you just got ditched. So sorry, man."

"I think I should go," I said.

"Dude no, stay. Keep playing. Forget about her."

"Thanks but I better go," I said as I slowly shuffled off into the night.

Not long after Hill and I went back to the trendy bar on a bitterly bleak and mercilessly cold winter's weeknight. When we arrived the red velour ropes were out, but no one was waiting. Just an overweight middle-aged man with glasses, dressed in a parka asking to be let in. The Bouncer quickly admitted us and as I walked in I heard him say: "You have to wait there." To which the man replied: "But why can't I just come in? The place looks empty!"

We were not there for more than half an hour when Hill came up to me as I was unsuccessfully trying to get the phone number of a German graduate student, visibly upset and demanding to leave.

The car ride home was deadly silent for a few minutes, then she burst out and confessed to me that the coat check attendant she had the hots for was now seeing a waitress at the bar. And a tall, thin, pretty, blonde "shiksa" type (as Hill described her) at that.

"Y'know what? I like, totally don't ever want to go there again. Omigod, that place, like, so sucks. It's, like totally for douchebags."

"Yeah," I replied, "I was thinking the same thing. It's still not too late. Let's go for a hot caffeinated beverage at *Le Figaro*. My treat."

"For sure. Like, totally," she said.

SUPERSTITION IS NOT THE PROPER MEANS OF GETTING THINGS DONE

Late one October I paid a visit to The Weasel. While he was taking care of some business matters on the phone, I sat in the dining room with his very pregnant wife, and their two young sons. The boys had their crayons out and were colouring some Halloween pictures.

The older of the boys turned a page in his colouring book, revealing a cartoon drawing of a pointy-tailed, pitchfork bearing devil. His mom was taken aback.

"Don't colour that picture," she told her son. "I don't want you to have anything to do with that picture. Its bad luck!" And she meant it, quickly ripping the page out and tossing it in the trash.

I find it foolish that people would dread something as benign as a cartoon drawing in a child's colouring book. To me it's like teaching children to fear and avoid other figures from fiction like Darth Vader or Sauron. I wanted to reassure the boys that there is no such thing as The Devil; that he is but a mere creation of man's imagination; a merging of his fear of the unknown and unforeseeable, dreamt up to scare people into maintaining the status quo and teach the masses not to question authority. I wanted to tell the boys that organized religions only exist to perpetuate themselves. I wanted to tell them that it was okay to colour every page of their little books, and no harm would come to them as a result. But I knew I had no right to tell her how to raise her kids in a house where I was a mere guest, so I kept my mouth shut.

The Weasel and his wife are probably the two most superstitious people I know. It is one thing to find a penny on the street and pick it up thinking it will bring you good fortune. I mean, we all have our little quirks and idiosyncrasies, but they almost live their lives by these bizarre rules. For example, she never accepts anything from anyone under a doorway, believing it will mean they will one day be enemies, which I am told is an old Eastern European superstition. (I once ran into an author on a stairway at work, and he immediately said his grandmother told him never to trust anyone you meet in a stairwell. I informed him that we had met previously on a level surface, which seemed to reassure him. We did not go on to be friends, so I guess this is at best a moot point.)

On a trip the three of us took to Atlantic City back before they were married, The Weasel was on a winning streak at a blackjack table. It was getting late, and his soon-to-be better half went to fetch him so we could leave. The second she showed up, he started to lose.

"Get outta here … you're bad luck!" he, in all seriousness, said to the love of his life. Immediately after she left, understandably angrily, The Weasel started to win again, so maybe he was correct.

I was with them on a particular Christmas Eve years ago. Their young boys had spent the day working on a watercolour painting as a gift for Santa Claus. After placing it by the fireplace, they went to bed. They had also left some cookies and a glass of milk for Santa, and some carrots.

"Why the carrots?" I asked.

"They're for the reindeer."

"Reindeer don't eat carrots!" I said. "Where would they find them on the arctic tundra? Was this your idea or the kids?"

She replied with: "They wanted to leave something for the reindeer, and I heard somewhere that reindeers eat carrots."

"And where did you hear that?"

"Oh, brother! Forget about the stupid carrots, Andre! Nobody cares! Why do you always have to be such a pain in the ass? See? See? This is why no woman in her right mind would want to date you, let alone fuck you! Forget about that, okay? I have an assignment for you: Write a thank-you letter from Santa for the kids, y'know, thanking them for the cookies and carrots. Say something like: 'I loved the cookies they were delicious, thank you and Rudolf loved the carrots.' Y'know, something like that!"

"But reindeer don't eat …"

"Oh, just shut and do it already. Sheesh!"

Of course I obliged her, because one of my few fond childhood memories involves my parents fooling my brother and me into thinking Santa ate the Oreo cookies and drank the milk we left for him. At the time my brother and I were about the same age as their boys. And talk about Christmas miracles: In order to pull it off, my parents would've had to have worked as a team!

So I wrote the little thank you note, and she and I stood by the fire The Weasel had just lit trying to decide what to do with the cookies, carrots, and adorable painting the boys made. She wanted to keep the painting, but feared that the curious boys would discover it in the future, blowing the whole deal, and then she and her husband would have some explaining to do. In the middle of discussing this, The Weasel, without word or warning, grabbed the cookies, carrots and painting, and threw them onto the fireplace, where they immediately burned up.

"What the hell!" she shouted.

The Weasel turned to his wife, looked her straight in the eye, and in a deadpan voice said: "It's bad luck to keep anything that's supposed to go to Santa!"

Believe it or not, she instantly accepted that as fact. I, on the other hand, was slightly more sceptical.

"You know, Santa doesn't really exist, eh?" I said.

"I know," The Weasel answered.

"And where exactly did you hear about this ritual? Was it from the same person who told you reindeer eat carrots?"

When he answered with: "It just is!" I knew he had made that one up on his own. To be fair, there is no reason why his rules would be any better or worse than anyone else's.

The Weasel probably got his superstitious streak from his mother, who claimed she could read one's future in the rings left over after drinking a cup of Greek coffee. She also had a book from the old country that had a code for answering questions with beans. Yes, *beans*. One would ask from a list of questions in the first part of the book, then randomly grab a series of finger-fulls of beans from a bowl. You counted how many beans you pulled each time, for example: 4-3-4-6, and you looked it up in the book. It would provide some ambiguous answer, although other times it was a little more direct. We were doing a fortune telling session one evening with The Weasel, his sister, his mom, Stretch and myself. Stretch chose the question: "Will the girl I marry be a Virgin?" (Something apparently so important in Greece that it had to be in this book.) His answer translated as: "A Virgin only in the heart."

A week later I was at The Weasel's home again for a New Year's Eve dinner. Overall 2006 was not one of my favourite years. I was anxious to see it come to a close, and The Weasel knew this, which is probably why he invited me over. Also attending were his two brothers-in-law and their respective wives and children, and his mother-in-law, a diminutive and aged Eastern European. Altogether, there were thirteen of us at the table.

The mother-in-law was even more superstitious than our hosts combined, and was so fearful of dining at a table of thirteen that she threatened to leave the party.

"You should not have invited him! Why is he even here? He is not family! He will bring us bad luck! Doesn't he have a family of his own? He should go get his own family!" she said as she pointed a short, shaky finger at me while I sat right next to her.

I felt it best just to keep quiet and get through the evening without another incident. But somewhere between soup and salad, the mother-in-law dropped her full glass of red wine onto my lap.

"What the ..." I said as I stood up.

It felt as if 2006 was taking a final shot at me; what else could I do but laugh?

"Hey everyone! Looks like the drinks are on me!" I joked.

Crickets.

I guess they felt that corny old joke wasn't funny, or they thought I was making fun of their matriarch, or they didn't want me there either. Or maybe a combination of all that?

We finished dinner with my jeans in The Weasel's washing machine. He let me wear a pair of his designer sweatpants, which I took home with me and still retain.

"Don't worry," The Weasel said. "Someone spilling wine on you on New Year's Eve is a sign of good luck in the coming year!"

"Oh yeah," I said, "and where exactly did you hear that?"

He just shot me a wry smile.

THE GREAT WHITE HUNTER

I spent the better part of my working life in customer service. In that time I got to meet and converse with thousands of diverse people. Today there are few I remember, let alone think about. Olav (that is not his real name) is one I will never forget.

Olav was a tall, beefy man in late middle-age who spoke with a loud, gregarious Eastern European accent, was exceedingly friendly and generous with the staff and had a good sense of humour. He was in business with his son, who was, with the exception of the big personality, a clone of his father; they had a sort of Jango and Boba Fett kind of thing going on.

One day Olav and asked me to make an international money order for a substantial amount in South African currency to a company that had the words "safari" and "adventure" in its name. He also asked for a large amount in Rands, when most people wanted Euros. I informed him I could make the draft immediately, but the cash could take a week or so.

"It is okay," he said with a smile, "I do not leave until next month. Here," – he gave me his business card – "call me when they are in."

I did not really know how he earned a living; all I knew is that he and his son travelled often, mostly to somewhere in Europe. What he did gave me the creeps when I read his card: Polite, friendly, sociable Olav was an arms dealer.

A week or so later his South African cash arrived and I called Olav to let him know. He arrived post haste, and after giving it to him, he thanked me with his usual amiable smile and gave me a $20 tip.

About two months later Olav came by holding an envelope of developed pictures from his trip. He was all too eager to share its contents with me.

The first was a picture of him dressed up like a chubby Stuart Granger complete with brown leather boots, holding a wooden-stock bolt-action hunting rifle with a scope, and crouching next to a beautiful zebra.

"How did they get the zebra to kneel like that? Is it trained?" I asked.

"Oh it's not kneeling, it's dead," he said proudly. "I shot it."

The next picture had him posing next to a small gazelle, dead as well. Then a wildebeest, also deceased. Then a newly killed gnu. And then something that made me wish I was blind: A photo of him, with a shame-fully self-satisfied grin, beside a huge dead maned lion.

"What no elephants?" was the only thing I could think to say.

"No, elephants are too expensive," he answered matter-of-factly. (To this day I'm not sure if he was kidding or not.)

He told me that there is huge piece of savannah land in South Africa where they built a 5-star luxury hotel. They breed most of the animals for rich jerks to hunt. Some others are tagged and carefully monitored in the wild, later to be marked for death because they are sick or too old to mate. But it was not a real safari; many of the animals were released specifically for the hunters, who chased them from safely inside a jeep. It made me wonder what they would do if they exhausted their supply of bullets? Run the animal over with the Range Rover? Use hand grenades? Land mines?

Each animal had a price. As it turns out, maned male lions were more expensive than female lions. It goes by demand, and most "great white hunters" want a fully grown male king of the beasts for their collection.

That is not sport, it's slaughter. People like that just want to kill things. How can this be fun for anyone, playing a game that's fixed? The beasts never had a chance to get away. The hunters didn't even camp out, and were themselves never in any kind of peril, unless they accidentally shot them-selves or drowned in the hotel pool after stuffing themselves at the buffet.

I asked him what they did with the animals after they were gunned down.

"Oh, they also provide a taxidermy service where they stuff and mount the animals, or make them into carpets of whatever. They will arrive here soon."

I guess that's why he didn't want to shoot a giraffe: It wouldn't fit in his house.

"And they give the meat to area poor people so they could eat. In fact, they cooperate with the local tribespeople who work as the guides," he said, as if he were trying to validate all this. "And they employ the locals at the hotel as well. It brings quite a bit into the economy. And it helps with wildlife conservation."

Even if it did all that, it still made me uncomfortable.

As if all the gold and diamond mines in South Africa were not enough. I became certain Olav would have found a way to do this regardless.

As if murdering them in an unfair fight were not enough, he also had mocking photographs taken and then used their corpses to decorate his home, which I imagine is some kind of sad, macabre museum of animals he has slain; all this from someone who got rich off of human misery. This guy was a nut bar with almonds.

It is somewhat hypocritical for me to claim to be disgusted with the act of hunting animals, not only because I eat meat, but because from the time I was nine years old my father took my brother and I out on hunting trips. But that was different. Most often we never found any game and just shot paper targets or tin cans. And for us it was a family tradition. My mom even came along. My father used to go hunting with his father, and a big part of it was just being in the outdoors. The animals were wild and had a fair chance to escape, and often did. There was sport in it. It was fair. And what's more we did not stuff and mount our quarry in some humiliating fake pose; we ate whatever we killed.

Some of my fondest childhood memories involve Sundays in the autumn when we would go out hunting; beside the movies, sojourns to closed commercial establishments, and the occasional beach trip, it was one of the few things we did as a family. At first I was too young to actually hunt. Quebec law at the time you said had to be at least twelve, but for me that was okay. I was never really into killing things. As a city boy I didn't take to crawling around in the forest through mud and over swamps like my father and brother. I would usually stay behind at the car with my mom, plucking the dead birds before she disembowelled them and placed them in a cooler. If they were still alive she would efficiently snap their neck with a quick twist of her hand. It may seem brutal, but that is how all meat is prepared. My mother, who grew up on a very rural farm, was adept at butchering animals.

I was seven the first time I visited my grandmother's house in Greece. Mom told me stories of the family farm and I, who had not yet been to her homeland, imagined a farmhouse like *The Waltons* had; I arrived unprepared for what I saw. It was a two-room white adobe-like house constructed on a sloping hill; it had no glass windows, electricity or indoor plumbing, and was built on top of the coop that housed my grandmother's live poultry and rabbits.

On the first evening there, my grandmother asked Mom to prepare a chicken. So she got a hatchet and a stick that looked like a small shepherd's crook. I accompanied her, totally ignorant as to what was about to happen. Mom asked me to select a live chicken. I chose a beautiful, fat, white and grey one. She immediately grabbed it with the crook and beheaded it with the hatchet on a tree stump in a swift, smooth motion. It happened so quickly I just stood there, frozen in shock. Then as a joke she threw the chicken's headless body at me. It was still moving frantically, which was scary as hell. I jumped and screamed.

Mom thought this was hilarious. Growing up where she did with no refrigeration animals like chickens, rabbits, pigs and goats had to be killed and butchered almost daily in order to eat, so I guess developing a sense of humour about it helped her deal with the ugliness. For her it was a matter of survival. She collected the befallen fowl once it settled down, which was, believe me, long before I had settled down and had it plucked, prepared and roasting in the wood-burning oven within a few minutes. Mom had not been on the farm for over twenty years, but it was like she never left.

My mother's attitude towards slaughtering her own supper best displayed how she could at times be a contradictory and complex person. Killing a chicken or a game bird was nothing to her, but when one of her budgies died, she practically gave it a funeral. She buried it at a local park, and set up two small sticks in a cross atop the tiny mound that was its grave, as if the bird in question was a Christian. When Mom was growing up Easter was a time she dreaded. Greeks, in a barbaric voodoo-like ritual, kill the first lamb born in the spring to celebrate Christ's resurrection. Because she always felt sorry for the young creature, as well as its mother, who would continue in vain to call out for its offspring, my mom would refuse to eat at the holiday feast, much to the amusement of her siblings, who openly ridiculed her for that.

After my parents split up we never went hunting again, although my brother, more the outdoorsman than I ever was, still participates in that activity as well as fishing.

Today there are hunting lodges (in the States) where the birds are bred and placed in cages waiting to be released in the path of hunters. They even have deer hunting where the unfortunate beasts are lured to automatic feeders as the hunters lie in wait in camouflaged shelters, and other places where larger animals, sometimes even domesticated goats, are released in a fenced-in area for "hunters" to pick off one by one, sometimes with military-style rifles. If my father ever saw guns like the military-style AR-15's or AK-47's used for hunting today he would laugh.

"Ahh, that *eez not* hunting," he'd probably say, "*efta enai malakiess.*" [Loosely translates to 'That's ridiculous bullshit!']

I haven't seen Olav in a long time. I sometimes wonder if he ever saved up enough money to bag an elephant. He probably did; sadly, no one has ever gone broke selling arms.

THE MERRY MONK

One autumn The Weasel got a new job that required him to attend an intense eight-week training course in Toronto. The company was generous enough to rent him a small bachelor condo in the entertainment district. During that time he was able to score a couple of good tickets to a Habs/Leafs exhibition game at the Air Canada Centre (as it was called at the time), and when he told me this, I was there. (Come to think of it, he never really asked me if I wanted to go. I immediately said "I'm in!" and he didn't contradict me. Did he intend to ask someone else like his brother-in-law?) He told me to get to Toronto by a certain date. I chose the train, because of its affordability and its downtown-to-downtown in 4 hours service. Becoming a bit of a Weasel myself, I coerced him into buying me an airline ticket so we could fly back together. (And in doing so, I could get a free ride home from the airport as well. Hurray for Andreas!)

I worked until midnight the day before departing, and since my train left at 6:30 a.m., I decided to stay up all night. I tried to sleep on the train ride over, but a bloated businessman-type guy sitting behind me spent all his time either blabbing obnoxiously loud on his phone, or snoring like a chainsaw as he slept. I felt like grabbing a pillow and smothering the oversized bastard.

I arrived at the condo around 11:30 a.m. The Weasel had left a key for me with the doorman.

At last, some sleep!

Or so I was foolish enough to believe. The building in question was having a new fire alarm system installed, and they kept testing it every five minutes. At around 2 in the afternoon, upon finally reaching sleep, I was rocked out of bed when they were considerate enough to blast an announcement that they were finally finished with the alarm testing for the day.

Thanks for letting me know, assholes!

The Weasel conveniently forgot to bring any Montreal Canadiens apparel, so there I was, alone with my huge, red vintage Habs jersey. I certainly turned a few heads. I stood out like a big, fat, target. The ticket-scanner was a nice older woman who kidded me about not being allowed admission because I was wearing the wrong colour. I sat next to a nice, elderly gentleman at the game who was a life-long Toronto Maple Leafs fan. He was so old he could remember when they won the Stanley Cup in '67! (There was that kind kidding between us, but it was entirely amicable.) The real problems came after the game, which the Habs lost, as we walked back to the condo. We had to pass by the Skydome, just as a Blue Jays game was ending.

It was then I had an encounter with one of the Jays fans. He was a thin man in a Canadian tuxedo and a baseball cap which concealed his mullet, and possibly that he was balding. He had wispy facial hair and looked to be in his late twenties.

"Hey!" he called out. "The Habs suck!"

A poet, no less!

I quickly turned around, much to the dismay of The Weasel, who feared I would start some kind of melee in which we would both get pummelled. I didn't think it likely. I was more than twice the guy's size. I walked right up to him and said: "I've been to eight Stanley Cup parades in my lifetime! How many have *you* been to?"

He had nothing further to say.

"Eight! In my lifetime!" I added as I marched away, holding up eight fingers.

The street was lined with school buses full of kids leaving the ballgame. One of the kids, who looked to be about twelve, opened his window and shouted to me from the safety of his seat: "Hey, Frenchy!"

Frenchy?

I immediately turned my unfriendly eyes towards him as he awkwardly tried to close the school bus window. When he was unable to do so, he quickly hid under his seat until I walked away.

It must be said, though, that most of the baseball fans were a little friendlier, and just asked what the final score was or what happened at the game.

Closer to the condo, The Weasel and I ran into a group of white trash looking lowlifes who were openly drinking beer on the street. One of them stumbled up to me.

"A Canadiens shirt? That's a go where I come from!" he spat at me through his wire-brush mustache.

"Oh yeah? What trailer park is that?" I said.

The Drunk's friends laughed. He was at a loss for words, but then again, he probably only knew a few to begin with. He turned around, and walked away giving me the old two-hand "Forget you! You're not worth it!" wave. Most people do that to save face, and make it seem like they got the last word. I let the whole matter drop, and walked away knowing I'm the one who came out ahead, even if the Habs didn't that night. We slipped into Wayne Gretzky's Sports Bar on Blue Jays Way for a drink, and my attire stopped the party and silenced the room upon our arrival. We didn't stay long.

The next day I saved for a lunch with an old college friend: A massive wall of a man, the loquacious Solomon Fiscus. He was born in Montreal, but moved to T.O. after university, and makes a living in television post-production and as a feature-film editor and director. I had only seen him once since his wedding five years earlier, although we regularly kept in touch via e-mail correspondence and phone calls.

We agreed to meet at his favourite Thai restaurant on Church Street, which appropriately enough had a lot of churches on it. I can't remember what the place was called ... I think it was *Thai a Yellow Ribbon* ... or maybe it was *Thunder Thai's* ... no, that's not it, either ... Hmmm, was it *Thai Me Up, Thai Me Down*?

As it turned out I was about half an hour early, so I decided to do a little exploring up the aforementioned street. About a block north I found an old-fashioned novelty store the likes of which I had not seen since I was a boy. I thought those kind of shops had gone the way of the dodo long ago. I checked out the window display.

I have to tell Fiscus about this! He'll flip!

His father used to own a similar store on St. Laurent Boulevard in Montreal decades earlier. Then I thought that he probably already knew about the shop, so I decided to visit it myself after lunch.

Everything went well, and it was great to see Fiscus again. The meal was good; the talkative giant is an excellent raconteur, and regaled me with interesting and amusing insider anecdotes of the productions and famous actors he had worked on over the last few years.

I eventually I told him about the store, and he had no idea it was there. Fiscus was just as excited as I was about seeing the place. He asked me if I had been inside. I told him no and asked why he wanted to know. As it turns out, he was interested in buying a novelty his father used to sell in his store called *The Merry Monk* and to his surprise I knew exactly what that was.

The Merry Monk is a six-inch cheap plastic bobble-head monk made in Hong Kong. What makes him so "merry" is that when you press down on his bald head, a long erect penis pops out of his robes.

Visiting the store was not unlike stepping into a time capsule. They even had a wall of sunglasses exhibited on cheap, seventies-style cardboard hangers. Fiscus, with the wonderment of a child, said his father's shop had the exact same display hung the exact same way.

He struck up a conversation with the store's owner, a pleasant woman in her forties as I checked out her inventory of clear plastic water pistols, Groucho glasses, fake dog shit and rubber vomit. We ended up talking to her for quite some time. It turns it they've been in business since the 1930's, the entire time in the same family. And when Fiscus mentioned he was in the film industry, the store's owner mentioned that TV shows and movies filmed there all the time.

At one point I asked to see a novelty Oscar trophy, and upon clutching it I launched into an over-the-top acceptance speech that brought the house down.

I mentioned to the owner that the only thing the store lacked was an old, bald, short, chubby guy with enormous, thick glasses and a cigar who would tell stories about how in 1936 he had a smoked meat sandwich and coffee at the Brown Derby in Montreal, and got change back from his nickel.

"Oh, we had someone like that here, minus the cigar," the owner said. "My grandmother. She died a few years ago but that was exactly what she was like." She then showed me a photo of her grandmother with Matt Damon, of all people.

We told her that she should get a website and sell some of these things on the internet. Novelty shops like hers are a rarity, and there are loads of people out there who would pay top dollar for that kind of kitschy stuff, but she informed me she already had that business.

As it turned out, they had several *Merry Monks*. Fiscus paid for his and we were about to leave when I asked the store's owner for her business card. She said she didn't have one, "unless you want our old card from the 50's."

"Are you kidding!?!" I shouted. "What is it about the conversation we had for the last hour that'd lead you to believe I wouldn't want a card from the 50's? I'd want that over any new one!"

The large, dusty, and faded business card was two sided, with an old-style phone number (ELGIN 4519) on the top corner. I wish now that I had asked for several more.

It is experiences like that one – unplanned and simple – that tend to be the most meaningful to me. I went for a grandiose, expensive NHL exhibition game, and instead it's a simple, sentimental, unexpected visit to an anachronistic novelty shop that now echoes in my memory the loudest.

I met up with The Weasel for an early supper before catching our flight back to Montreal. We went back to Wayne Gretzky's for dinner on the rooftop dining area, and found we were the only ones there. Before ordering we were approached by a pair of attractive, flirtatious young women. They seemed almost too attractive. As it turns out they were reps from a popular American brewery and they were there to get us to drink their brand of beer. Or more accurately, they were trying to get The Weasel to try their new beer. They completely ignored me. And when I tried to say something, they quickly glanced at me as though I were annoying them and then immediately back at him in a motion so blatant that both The Weasel and I laughed at their nerve right in front of them.

After they left us he said: "Man! Even women who are paid to be friendly don't want anything to do with you!"

As if that needed to be pointed out.

20 LBS. OF FLOUR

As a youth I never had issues with my back. I grew up straight and strong, without having engaged in any sport more rigorous than bike-riding and doing my best to avoid injury. My problems began in my early twenties, when on a Sunday afternoon in autumn, an SUV ploughed into my tiny Toyota Tercel hatchback, turning a sub-compact into a sub-sub-compact, totalling the aforementioned vehicle with me inside. The quick, unexpected crunch of glass and metal snapped my seat back and twisted my body like a French cruller. Thankfully I was able to walk away with no more immediate damage than a sore back and neck. The discomfort soon enough went away, but the effects lingered, recurring every so often. The worst attack happened at work on an autumn Thursday. While lifting a box of books, I felt a small tingle in my lower back. Within 45 minutes I could not sit down, and a half hour later I was in such terrible agony that I could barely walk.

I had to leave work early with no realistic plan for getting home. I called everyone I knew, but it being the middle of the afternoon on a weekday all my friends and family were otherwise engaged. I finally decided to try and make my way to a hospital. As I stepped out onto McGill College Avenue, the distance across the street to the taxi stand suddenly became a great, impassable expanse. I carefully lurched forward as best I could when one of my calls was returned; a friend of mine was on her way downtown to pick up her husband, an elderly college professor whose hip was a few weeks away from being replaced, and could come and get me as well.

When she arrived I tried to crawl into the backseat of her car.

"Hey, I'm not a chauffeur," she said. "You can sit up front!"

She relented after I explained that for me sitting was out of the question. After we picked up her husband, I asked her to drive me to the hospital.

"There's nothing they can do for you there. I know these things," she said, with her husband, no stranger to the agonies of the lower back pain himself, agreeing with her.

"They'll only give you anti-inflammatories and send you home. I'll take you to a pharmacy, we'll get something for the pain, and then I'll take you home."

"You don't have to stay! Just please, leave me at emergency," I said.

After she dropped her husband off at their place, she drove me to a pharmacy. I asked her to buy me a particular medication, and gave her the money. As I lay in the backseat of her small sedan waiting, I was noticed by several people as they walked past the car. They looked at me as though I were a potential kidnapper, waiting to pounce on an unsuspecting victim.

My friend returned to the car and handed me a bag.

"Here you go. Your change is inside."

"Hey, this isn't what I asked for," I said.

"Oh, these are better."

"But I wanted ..."

"I said these are better!"

They weren't.

The next day the crippling agony had increased tenfold and again I was on the phone imploring my friends to take me to the hospital. Finally I called my father, himself a veteran of several spinal surgeries. I knew he would help me.

"No, just rest at home and the pain will go away," he said. "I know these things."

Only after serious begging and imploring did he agree to take me to a doctor on Monday if the pain persisted.

After an agonizing weekend that had me staying mostly in bed, Monday morning came and the torturous misery was worse to the point where my diminutive, octogenarian father had to act as my cane, no easy task for him considering I weigh enough to qualify as a sumo wrestler.

"Why didn't you tell me *eet* was so bad?" he said.

He took me to a large clinic he frequented with his innumerable geriatric health issues. It was located in the same shopping mall where a group of Greek seniors rent a small space to hang out. I think he chose to bring me there so he could play cards and backgammon and drink coffee with his friends while I waited to see a doctor.

The clinic was packed. My number was 56 and they just called 22. The ugly orange plastic seats in the waiting room were moulded, making it impossible for me to lie down across several of them. After standing uncomfortably for over an hour I realized that, while there were only two doctors on hand, the clinic had fourteen examination rooms, so I asked the receptionist if I could please lie down in one of their vacant rooms, making it clear that I was more than willing wait my turn to see a physician.

The receptionist sighed loudly as she explained that there were people ahead of me and I had to wait. Obviously she didn't get what I was saying, so I repeated: "Look, I'm not demanding to see a doctor right away, it's just that my back is hurting so much and I need to lie down in the meantime. I will wait for my number, just please … the pain … it's too much!"

She sighed even louder and gave me a bitter, unfriendly glare that said "what a whining baby" before angrily gesturing for me to follow her, leading me to an unoccupied examination room where I was instructed to wait. She quickly exited, slamming the door behind her. I heard her muffled voice tell the doctor just outside the room that I demanded to see someone right away.

The doctor stormed in and gave me a stern lecture about how I was being unfair to the others and that I should wait like everyone else. When I tried to explain that I was willing to do just that I only needed a place to lie down, he would have none of that and angrily waved his hand in a "silence, you!" fashion and told me to lie face-down on the examination table. After obeying him he proceeded to yank and bend my legs in different positions.

"Does this hurt?" he said coldly.

"Owww, yes."

"How about this?"

"Yes!"

"How about –"

"Look," I said, "it always hurts a great deal no matter what."

"Fine. I'll have some X-rays taken," he said, stomping out of the room.

As I struggled to get off of the table, the radiologist, a small, older woman with thick glasses, entered.

"Oh, you poor man," she said. "Let me help you."

As we made our way to the X-ray room, everyone else in the office stared at her. One of the nurses walked up to her, whispered something in her ear. Instantly the radiologist turned unfriendly.

After examining the X-rays the doctor wrote me a prescription and a worker's comp chit, telling me there was no visible damage to my spine and I should go home, rest, and return to see him again in a week.

It took me about half an hour to make what should have been a casual stroll to where my father was playing cards. He asked me to wait until he finished his game of *xeri* and coffee before we left.

It was to be the longest seven days of my life. It took me the better part of an hour to get out of bed each morning. Every task from going to the bathroom to preparing meals was torture. And the worst part: I was all by myself day and night, with only my smartphone and social media for company. I communicated mostly with my friend Liz in Toronto via Facebook, but for some reason she would only correspond with me from 9 to 5, Mondays to Fridays, as if she only checked her FB page while she was at work.

Sleep was the most difficult task. I would take two nighttime pain pills and lie in bed on my side, with my knees bent using three pillows: One under my head, one between my legs, and hugging a third one. (When I told one of my co-workers about this, she said while laughing "That's how pregnant women sleep!") I slowly shifted and carefully adjusted myself until I was in the ideal position, free of pain. But after a while, lying there would inevitably become uncomfortable. My arm either went numb or my shoulder became sore, so I had to roll over, which would take several agonizing minutes. I would begin by gently straightening my legs. (One false move could trigger another horrible, crippling spasm.) Once that was done I would gingerly, inch by inch, try to roll over onto my back. If that went without incident, I would lie there, breathing heavily, anticipating the possible pain that could occur on the second half of this maneuver. A last deep breath and then I would continue the roll, cautious not to move my hips too far or twist my back, and eventually set myself in position. The final, and most perilous stage, would be readjusting the pillows. This process would be repeated a couple of times a night.

I called my father and asked him for some provisions, requesting specific items. He brought me an extra-large carton of eggs wrapped in newspaper and tied with twine, like the kind you get from a farmer's market, butcher-sliced slabs of bacon and ham, and a 20-pound bag of flour, none of which were on my list.

"What the hell is all this?" I said.

"What?" my father said. "My mother fed our entire family of eight for a month with that during the Depression! You kids today you are so ungrateful!"

"*Kids?*" I was over forty by then.

This is not atypical behaviour for my father. He is quite stubborn and old-fashioned. He believes that every situation calls for actions that were only appropriate in Greece in the 1930s, as if humanity had achieved its pinnacle, reached ultimate perfection, an epoch-shattering apex, in that time and place. For example he always drinks his coffee black, a habit he certainly picked up when he was a young man in Greece when, after World War II, cow milk and sugar were expensive luxuries. Every time he notices me putting two creams and two sugars in my cup of java he looks at me disappointingly, probably thinking: "What did I raise, a Nancy-boy!?!" My father also orders his steaks "well-done," hating to have any trace of pink inside, and he ingests every bit of it, including the fat, which he refers to as "the best!" I can't describe the level of disapproval on his face as I order my steak "medium" and leave the fat on the side of my plate.

I learned not to waste a trip anywhere in my apartment. If I had to, say, go to the bathroom, I would use the excursion to wash the dishes, prepare a meal, refill my drink, and get several other things done. More than once it took so long to rise that, by the time I was on my feet, I had forgotten what I had intended to do.

In between high-cholesterol meals with unleavened bread I would text friends in an attempt to get them to visit me if only to break the mind-numbing monotony of *Star Trek* re-runs, CNN news cycles, and back-to-back-to-back broadcasts of the reality crime show *First 48*. My brother passed by one night with a rented DVD, but that was about it.

The next Monday I returned to the doctor. He was smiling when he entered the examination room; a smile that turned to a frown the second he saw it was me again. The medication was working and I had improved, but not enough to return to work, so I was given an additional week of rest. Before long my father returned me to my hermitage for another round of cabin fever.

My only houseguest that week was The Weasel, whom I had to prod, cajole and guilt into seeing me. I asked him if he could pick up two litres of cranberry juice and some bagels. (There is a 24-hour bagel shop, where he could quickly and easily get the aforementioned items, directly between his house and my apartment.) He showed up an hour and a half later than he said he would with an opened, three-quarter full bottle of orange juice and a bag of frozen supermarket bagels, the kind with raisins which he knew I hated. He probably grabbed said items from the refrigerator in his cold room on his way out the door. The whole time he was over he kept looking at his watch, and left after less than an hour.

If the first week was the longest in my life, the second was even longer. The world seems different when one is home on a weekday. You become familiar with daytime TV, radio, and the habits of your neighbours. I was especially surprised to discover how many times a day someone knocked on my door. By the time I got up to answer, they were usually gone, so I never found out who they were.

I was still a little sore the third time I saw the doctor, but I lied and said I was perfectly fine. I could not take another week of isolation. He let me return to work and gave me a note for my boss that stated clearly that I was to avoid any lifting for two weeks.

"Is there anything I can do to prevent a repeat of this?" I asked.

The doctor shrugged.

"What if I bought a back brace of some kind?"

"Okay, sure, why not," he said.

Was this joker really a doctor?

So I bought a back brace. All it did was squeeze my intestines like a tube of toothpaste and altered my bathroom habits.

The day I returned to work I didn't get a special welcome, not that I expected one, but it would have been nice if somebody said they missed me or that they were glad I was back, but nobody said it was nice to see me, or even inquired how I was. One co-worker wryly asked if I enjoyed my vacation, but otherwise it was like I never left. Whenever I asked someone to lift a heavy object for me, they would sigh loudly as they shot me a snarky look that said: "I'm lifting this for you, jerk! I had to do your job for two weeks, and now I still have to do it! Why didn't you just stay home! You owe me now!"

Ah, so good to be back.

NEW YEAR'S DAY WITH A DICTATOR

During Grade 7 my father gave me and my brother a ride to school every morning. Sometimes I would get to his cab first. Sometimes my brother. Sometimes my father. When I would go ahead of them my dad would let me turn over the ignition.

One cloudy and cool morning in early spring I went down alone and started the old Chevy Malibu Dad used as his taxi. I sat up front, one of the advantages of getting there ahead of my brother, patiently waiting and looking around. I'll never forget that moment: Between the driver's and passenger's seat was a court document labelled "Petition for Divorce."

My initial reaction was that some fare my father had the day before left it there.

No, it couldn't be? Could she finally be doing it? After all these years it is really going to happen?

My mother, in a fit of rage, would often say that she was going to divorce Dad. But I always thought it was an idle threat. She could really lose her temper, often so badly that the veins in her neck would swell to frightening proportions, and threaten a number of things that she never followed through with after she settled down, which was like watching The Hulk turn into Bruce Banner; in fact, like the aforementioned comic book metamorphosis, she would be usually oblivious to what she had said or did while upset.

Their marriage was nothing short of a train wreck; in fact, I sometimes wonder how it lasted as long as it did. It was the centrepiece of my nightmarish childhood, living in a household that could explode at any time.

It was so bad that my mother got a nighttime job at a bakery so she and my father could spend as little time with each other as possible. That farce of a "civil" union was so unpleasant that growing up I could not conceive in my mind the idea of a married couple getting along. And I believed all families were like ours. In Grade 2 I had a hippie teacher named Tina, whose last name I can't recall. One day she read an A.A. Milne *Winnie the Pooh* story to the class, afterwards telling us that she had such a large collection of *Pooh* books and memorabilia at home that it drives her husband crazy. Of course in my mind I immediately imagined him yelling something like: "I am so fucking sick of you and your stupid *Winnie the Pooh* books, you fucking bitch!" as he pulled the volumes off their shelves and threw them across the room. Her reply would be: "I hate you, you bastard! Go to hell!"

This was even more unbelievable when I met her husband, a post-Beatles John Lennon knock-off, right down to the circular granny-glasses, who probably spent most of high school being shoved into lockers. In reality their relationship was probably more like: "Another *Pooh* book? Honey, we are running out of room. Can't you please slow that down?" And she would reply: "Oh, you silly goose you, I'm sure by now you're aware that will never happen." You know, the kind of behaviour sane, normal people displayed.

On the drive to school my father told us that they were getting a divorce and he would be moving out on July 1ˢᵗ. Still, it should not have been such a surprise; they had been sleeping in separate beds for months. I could not understand why he would be staying until then. How could he do that? We lived in a small 5 ½ room flat. One bathroom. They could not avoid each other. Ultimately that period was the quietest, but most tension filled of their marriage.

Dad dropped us off in front of Outremont High and drove off. I stood on the curb for a moment, shocked. As I turned I saw that Peter had already headed inside without saying a word. He didn't want to talk about it. We still never have.

After my parents divorced in 1983 my brother and I would spend Christmas Day with our mother, and New Year's Day with Dad. While Mom usually made a traditional holiday turkey-centric feast, our father lacked the culinary skills to pull off such a feat, so instead he'd take us out for a large mid-afternoon meal, usually at an all-you-can-eat style buffet, accompanied by whomever he was married to at the time; and as if that were not awkward enough he would bring along his wife's daughter and her husband, and eventually their kids. They were decent people, but they never seemed enthusiastic about the get-together, and even skipped out of it a few times. It felt as if my father was trying too hard to force some kind of merger between our families. A sort of: "Look, our family didn't work out, but here is a nice one we can join! C'mon, they are way cooler!" (What really annoyed me about that was the way Dad acted like he had no role or responsibility in our family's dysfunction.) We were all uninterested in what felt like a shotgun wedding. They had other things to do and eventually they stopped coming altogether, and so did my father's wife, probably because of me. (For the record, I actually like my step-sisters and their husbands, and I would not have minded getting to know them better. I just would've preferred to do it on my own terms; to let the relationship happen organically.)

A few years ago we went to a restaurant in Laval, and I made the fateful mistake of not bringing my car, so I was completely at the mercy of my father and brother for a ride home. The party consisted of me, Dad, Peter, and my young nephew, Anthony. After lunch, we had to go back to Dad's place to see his wife. I have nothing serious against her really; she is a decent wife and companion to my father and is taking care of him in his final years. It is just more like severe, near fatal apathy. She has, on more than one occasion, told me to my face that she likes my brother more than me simply because every time he comes by their condo, he eats; the ingestation of nourishment being all that is required to get on this woman's good side. So by her standards, Mussolini is in heaven because he always cleaned off his plate. I knew I would be offered a Greek coffee that tastes like mud, which I would refuse, and offered stale, dry Greek flaky pastries, which I would also refuse, and then it'd begin. And to top it all off she has no sense of humour.

On this occasion my father's sister, who lives in the same building, was having a large gathering of friends and relatives, so of course we had to pass by and pay our respects. We were met at the door by my cousin Johnny B., whom I had not seen in more than a decade. He greeted me with: "How the fuck are you?" (A salutation not atypical for a Greek guy from Park Extension.) I was not offended; he meant well and it was agreeable to see him again. Johnny B. was there alone because he and his wife had split up that year, and she was somewhere else with their kids.

Among the many people present were my aunt's second husband and his daughter from his first wife, who was there with her husband, a moustached middle-aged man in a black shirt and matching beret. Both of them were on their second marriage as well. He looked like Saddam Hussein circa the first Gulf War; so much so that he had to be doing it on purpose. No one could possibly have looked like that by accident.

One of my uncles, my father's youngest brother, was in attendance as well with his second wife. He was once dashingly handsome (as a young man he dabbled in stage acting, specializing in playing characters who wore white turtlenecks); I remember as a small child my then bachelor uncle would spend the holidays with us because he had nowhere else to go. Now he was past retirement age and a grandfather himself; with his gigantic glasses on he looked a little like a Greek Larry King *sans* suspenders. And of course, in the centre of the table was the ubiquitous plate of olives and feta cheese.

We all sat down and drank and otherwise engaged in sparkling conversation. Peter was his usual silent self, but most everyone else was loud and lively. Many there had not seen me in years so a number of questions were pointed in my direction. I tried to be funny, cool and charming, but as is too often the case no one got anything I said.

Johnny B. dipped his hands into the olive plate and pulled one out, and started to wave it in front of me. He was trying to bait me, albeit playfully, but I would not go for it. I ignored him.

"Do you still hate these?" he said with a wry smile. "Remember when you were a kid you were afraid of these, eh?"

Well, I wasn't really "afraid" … more disgusted than anything else. And yes, I did. I readily admit to having the oddest eating habits of any human being alive. Odd in the sense that I find pickles disgusting and do not relish relish, but I love cucumbers, even though I know they are the same things. I hate raw tomatoes, but I love tomato sauce, ketchup, tomato based Italian cuisine, and so forth. Green peppers? No, thank you. Hot banana peppers? Not a problem! A number of Greek dishes also make me gag. *Pastichio*, often referred to as Greek Lasagna: Runny with a putrid aroma that turns me off before I sit at the table. There is another called *gimista*, which is hollowed out eggplants, tomatoes or green peppers stuffed with rice and meat; looks like someone ate a rice-based dish and defecated into vegetable scraps they dug out of the garbage. My brother can't get enough of either of those. Me? No thanks! And of course, my old adversary: The olive. Greeks feel the need to display those horrible things at every goddam meal. We would be having hot dogs. Hamburgers. Chinese food, for god's sake. And no matter what my parents would drag out those slimy, putrid oblong pellets.

There are two foods that Greeks love to gorge themselves on: olives and watermelons (what in Greek is called *karpusi*), both of which I cannot stand. I fail to comprehend how anyone could eat something that looks like it dropped out of a rodent's asshole; how they could bite into something soft with an impenetrable hard centre, and then separate the two in their mouths, spit that gross pit into their plates, and go on as if that was perfectly natural? And *karpusi*? Greeks bury their faces into them and pull away with a mouthful while the run-off drips down their chins, and then again they spit out the seeds. If you are chewing something and you need to spit it out, polite society insists you do that in a napkin. And I agree. You don't leave a gross half-chewed piece of meat on your plate during a meal. So why is it okay to spit out an olive pit or watermelon seed and let it just sit there on your plate?

However olive oil I have no problem with. In fact, I love olive oil.

You would think for once my parents would say: "Hey, why don't we *not* break out the olives and feta, just to make Andreas feel like he matters?" But no. It never even occurred to them. Not once.

My eating habits proved especially problematic for my parents when I was a child. When they entertained at home they could include dishes I liked, but when we went to other peoples' houses I would get fussy and difficult, leaving my parents embarrassed. More than once my father would take me out of the party and to a local restaurant to eat, or bring on outside food for me, something that was understandably considered rude and offensive.

"My mother slaved for two days to prepare a feast," a cousin loudly proclaimed while pointing a mean finger at me in front of everyone, "and this fuckin' guy won't eat!"

I eventually grew out of it … but not entirely.

Until I was ten I thought that my parents were not my real parents. I felt such a disconnect I imagined that as a newborn baby I was accidentally switched with another child at the hospital and one day my real mother and father, who were Hollywood movie stars, would come and claim me; take my back to tinsel town for an olive-free life of privilege. I was so deep into that idea that I would look carefully at actors who were the right age and scrutinized their eyes; if they were dark brown like my own, I would research them to see if they had any connection to Montreal.

Were they in town filming a movie and had a child born at the Jewish General Hospital? Could they be my real parents? Was there a place somewhere out there where I fit in?

I outgrew this fantasy, but for a long while it almost became an obsession.

The lively conversation continued for a while, then finally my aunt asked me why I was not yet married.

"Yeah, how come you're not married?" someone added.

"Yes, why don't you get married?"

"You really should!"

I sat silently, in disbelief.

I looked around the room and saw nothing but divorced people as far as the eye could see; I saw someone whose wife left him because his hair fell out; I saw someone who was blackmailed into his first marriage to someone who ultimately ended up institutionalized; I saw someone whose partner had a child with someone else while they were still married; I saw someone who was ruined financially by a split (they had agreed on child-support payments, and then she hired an asshole lawyer who said she could get more; she broke the verbal deal and sued, ruining her former partner financially and forcing him to lose his house); I saw people who were in abusive relationships; people who should know way better; people who had not learned a fucking thing with their experiences; people who should be encouraging me to fly solo. All of them have ended up in court, paying lawyers and judgements. Messy all the way. There is no such thing as a good break-up, or clean divorce. (Until then the only time I had ever been inside a courtroom was when The Weasel was called to testify in a case and I tagged along.)

"What's wrong with you people?" I yelled out, exploding. "Have you not been paying attention to your own lives? You've all gone through catastrophic marriages and now you want me to go through the same thing? What has to happen before you finally learn?"

Dead silence.

I sat ready to pounce. I was all set to let them all have it, one by one, like Jeannie C. Riley's mother (in song) giving the hypocritical (and metaphorical) Harper Valley P.T.A. their comeuppance. (A song that became a made-for-TV movie starring Barbara Eden, and subsequently an NBC sitcom, also starring Barbara Eden.)

I looked around at their stunned faces … and lost my nerve. They didn't mean any harm. They weren't trying to pry. They were just curious and conversational; trying to be friendly. Instead I just remarked that it was getting late and I had somewhere to go, and left. My brother, who probably wanted to go home more than I did, also excused himself, took his son, and departed with me, which was fortunate because he was my ride.

Once again Peter and I said nothing as he dropped me off at home. And I'm not waiting by the phone for any future invitations.

THE END ... AND A NEW BEGINNING

"Congratulations," she said.

"*Congratulations?" Really? Was she actually congratulating me? What the fuck!?! Is she being sarcastic? That would be unprofessional, wouldn't it?* I sat there in that small office, not sure what to make of this. *Since when is a positive diagnosis something one congratulates? Where did this begin? What brought me here?*

* * *

It began with yet another breakup. One more broken heart; one more time for the itsy-bitsy spider to again go up the water spout. But it actuality began a little after that, with the renewal of an older relationship. An ex-girlfriend named Danyka and what seemed like a chance encounter.

I didn't think I would ever see or hear from her again. The relationship had ended almost a decade before, and very badly. So badly that I figured she would slap me the next time she saw me and spit on the ground before me after what I called her when she ended us so abruptly, so coldly, and without explanation.

She was divorcing her husband, the guy she left me to marry because, as she put it, he had "more money, a better job and a better future" than I did. And now she wanted to see me again.

"Let's catch up. Over dinner," she said excitedly. "That would be great!"

We agreed to meet at a downtown gourmet burger joint we both knew. I braced for a tough night. It was Good Friday (the *faux* one). I showed up early, and didn't see her, so I decided to walk around, not being one to enjoy loitering on street corners. I was halfway up the block when I heard her call my name. Thinking I was leaving, she ran up the street full speed, slimmer than I remembered, with her reddish-brown hair now dyed platinum blonde, and into my arms for a big hug; it was like we never parted. The chemistry and the connection was still there. She later confessed that, eager to see me, she had arrived an hour earlier than we agreed. Over dinner I offered an apology for what I said years before.

"You don't have to be sorry. I deserved it," she said. "I should apologize to you, the way I treated you!"

No one had ever said anything like that to me before. Everyone made it seem like I was constantly at fault. Especially in relationships like ours.

Danyka went on to tell me that a few years earlier she was diagnosed with bipolar personality disorder, and that after trying a number of different drug therapies, some that made her even more manic, she finally found a medication that helps … sometimes.

That was it. The questions I had were answered in an instant. Everything about her behaviour made sense now.

After dinner we walked around downtown for a while and then hopped into her car and decided to go to *Le Figaro*, but we never made it there. Instead we went back to my place. We started up again that night and had a whirlwind affair. But we weren't dating. We would get take-out food or rent movies and stay over at each other's place, and even then only when *she* wanted to, never when I did. We saw each other once or twice a week for a few months, and communicated sporadically.

One day I woke up in her bed early on a Saturday morning. She wasn't there. I looked around her place to find Danyka lying on the living room couch, staring off into nowhere. When I called her name, she slowly turned her head to face me, and what I saw was not the happy, lively, humorous woman I knew and fell in love with years ago. Her eyes where in a tough squint, and her mouth was almost snarling. She didn't say a word. She just looked at me as if to say "Go away! Now!"

"Are you okay?" I asked.

Danyka didn't answer. She looked off, ignoring me. I don't know if she was hiding so that I would not see her like this, or maybe she just took her meds and they haven't kicked in yet. But I felt a chill. *Was that what she was like most of the time? Was that the reason she would only see me once or twice a week?*

I went back to bed. I woke up an hour later to find her in a manic state. *Perhaps she took too much of her meds this time?* She insisted that I leave. I don't want to go with her in that state, but she persisted and I didn't know what else to do, so I left. I called and texted her later that day and evening, to see if she was okay. She didn't reply until the next day, and said she was fine. When I asked to see her again she seemed almost embarrassed and kept putting it off. At first she would break dates; then she wouldn't return my calls, emails or texts. Then she totally ghosted me.

When I told The Weasel about this he said: "Sorry to say it looks to me like she was just using you to rebound with."

He was right. She just wanted the temporary reassurance of someone steady and caring and now Danyka was trying to unload me like a Betamax at a yard sale.

How could I have not seen this? I should have known!

During that time she started to sell or give away all her possessions. Eventually she returned one of my emails, and said that I deserved honesty and she felt that we had no real future. Then she ran off to Latin America to work in environmental conservation. I never saw or heard from her again.

Served me right. Should have learned my lesson the first time. I am always so critical of others who didn't take heed of their past mistakes, and now I was served a dish of cold, raw karma.

Why didn't I see this coming? Why do all my relationships fail? Why am I the way I am? What is it? WHAT IS IT!?!

Later that summer I was logging into my email system, which has a click bait news feed on the homepage. There in a bold letters I saw the headline:

"Singer Susan Boyle has Asperger's Syndrome"

I knew very little about Asperger's and autism at the time. Two of my cousins have sons with varying forms of autism: One so severe he can't even go to the bathroom by himself; the other dropped out of life after graduating college and spends almost all of his time alone in his room. From what I knew about it I was not sure what to think. Boyle didn't remind me of them, or anyone else I had encountered who was autistic. I read the article and soon forgot about it.

The next day, the same news feed had the headline:

"Dan Aykroyd Admits to Having Asperger's"

I had been watching Dan Aykroyd for years. Never would I have suspected. I also read that article. How could they have had that all their lives and no known, or suspected anything? At the end there was a link to a website where one could take an online test to see if they had it as well. I have often taken such tests as a lark. When I read *The Psychopath Test* by Jon Ronson, I took an online test and scored a 6 (a 20 or higher means you are a psychopath). No surprise. I didn't think that I was. I was just curious about the test.

So I took the Asperger's test. 50 questions. 30 or higher and you have it. The first question nearly knocked me out of my chair.

Question # 1: Do people often tell you that you are talking too loud?
Yes. A week doesn't go by where someone doesn't mention that.
Question #2: Do you walk with your head down?
Yes. Yes I do. I have always walked around looking at my feet.
Question #3: Do people often tell you what you just said was rude even though you insist it is not?
Yes. That happens all the time.

At that point I started to sweat.

Another Question: You prefer going to a museum rather than a play?
Yes. I prefer museums. Theatre's okay, but it's not something I go out of my way to attend.
Do you have trouble interacting with others?
Yes. All the time.
Do you prefer reading fiction or non-fiction?
If I read ten books, nine of them would be non-fiction.
Do you have your own strict moral code that you adhere to?
Well ... yeah.
Do your friends think you would make a good diplomat?
No!
When you talk on the phone are you unsure when it is your turn to speak?
Yes. That is why I am partial to texting or email.

Do you prefer to do things on your own or with others?
Holy shit!

After 50 questions my score was tabulated.
43!
I don't know how long I sat staring at my computer screen.
Could this be what's it's been all along?

Autism was the last thing I would have ever thought that I had. Was I really one of those people the kids in the schoolyard at Barclay used to call "retards?" I was nothing like Temple Grandin or my cousin's kids, or any of the other autistic people I have met or seen or heard of or seen in movies or TV; nothing like *Rain Man* … or was I?

I had to know.

I ordered a book called *The Complete Guide to Asperger's Syndrome* by Tony Attwood. When it arrived at work I quickly bought it, making sure no one saw me, and snuck it into my backpack. I started reading it during the bus ride home. The introduction included a fictional story about a boy named Jack that summed up my entire childhood. I had to fight to keep from tearing up right there. I soon finished the book, and while I had a number of traits and experiences listed in the volume, it still was not a perfect match. There were some aspects of Asperger's that did not fit me at all. Since a diagnosis was not covered by government insurance or the private health plan I had with my employer at the time, I had to be sure it was worth spending the significant amount of money it would cost.

I thought about my mid-twenties. After graduating Concordia and moving back home with my mother, who was recently divorced for the second time, I started a bit of a downward spiral. All those years of being in school rendered me emotionally exhausted, and I spent the summer just sitting around, staying up late, and sleeping in. Whenever I was home my bedroom door was closed. I took my meals there. With a TV in my room I almost never came out.

By Labour Day I found a part-time job at a record store that got me out and about, and it soon became a full time gig. But I was constantly stressed and anxious. Most mornings I would get out of bed and immediately throw up. Most evenings I would drink until I fell asleep. After pulling together enough to perform the best man duties at The Weasel's wedding, I found myself at the emergency room of the Royal Victoria Hospital. I had had enough. I needed answers.

A young psychiatrist named Dr. G with freakishly big brown eyes – eyes with irises that jutted so far out that I was surprised they didn't knock the glasses off her face – took me on and we began weekly sessions. She at first thought I had Obsessive-Compulsive Disorder. After further examinations and testing, she was able to eliminate that. Three months later she told me that I was not ill enough to continue with the sessions. She said if I bought a copy of *Feeling Good* by Dr. David M. Burns and read it that would help me more than therapy at the hospital.

"So, what do I have?" I asked.

"You don't really have anything serious," she said.

"So what? You're saying I'm neurotic?"

"Well, no. You're not, actually. Look, just get the book I told you, read it, do what it says and you should be okay."

"Are you sure?"

"Yeah, yeah, yeah … just do what I said," she said as she ushered me out the door.

I felt like I was getting dumped by another girlfriend.

So I did what she said and the book did actually help me. Also I started getting in Buddhism (although I never truly gave myself over to the tenets of The Enlightened One and fully converted) and other Eastern philosophies after reading about them in *Time* magazine, and that helped me get better as well. Finally, my mom bought me a dog. That gave me a sense of purpose, had me leaving my bedroom door open and got me out of the house and interacting with others. All three things slowly brought me back to life.

Around ten years later when I was working in financial services I started feeling rundown again and went to a private psychologist paid for by my work insurance. I didn't like or get along with him. He thought I had Attention Deficit Disorder, and when that proved not to be the case I quit going. I started feeling better anyway.

I didn't want this to be another dead end. But I had to keep pushing for a definite answer. So I went to Les.

Les and I have been good friends since we first met in Mark Blaker's *Third World Anthropology* class at Dawson College. Her first son was born with Down's syndrome, and so she chose a career as an elementary school teacher for special-needs children, most of her students being on the Spectrum. Few people on this planet know me as well as she does. We have no secrets. She would know.

We met for coffee and I recounted to her my story. After I finished, she stared at me and smiled. There was a long pause.

I felt like a fool. I knew she would say I was being silly and laugh at me.

"Andreas," she said slowly, as though choosing her words carefully, "this … explains … everything … about … you. You have this for sure."

"What!?!"

"You found your answer. You have this for sure."

"Well, why didn't you say something sooner?" I asked.

"I never made the connection. I was too used to you, I guess. But yeah, you are on to something here."

She really had no idea?

Just a few months earlier she called me and asked if I remembered the name of a summer fling she had when she was twenty and spent a few months out in British Columbia.

"Floyd O'Malley," I said without hesitation, despite not having thought about him since she showed me his picture upon her return from out west. I even remembered the photograph of Floyd in front of the forested B.C. coastline even though I had looked at it for just a few seconds. He was wearing a brown suede jacket and blue checkered shirt. His hair was black and parted on the left, and his eyes were blue. And Les was not surprised I would recall his name 24 years later? She *knew* I would know it. That's why she contacted me, and that was not enough to tip her off? That should have been a dead give-away something was up!

But ultimately she is not qualified to diagnose me. I had to find a way to get the money.

Things were a little tough then. My mother told me she had Multiple Myeloma. I couldn't tell her what I was going through. She wouldn't understand, and it would only upset her. My father would understand even less, and he was starting to show his age as well with Parkinson's disease and the onset of dementia that comes with it.

I went out for coffee with The Weasel at *Le Figaro*. We had not seen each other in a few months, and we were both eager to get caught up.

"Your mother has cancer?" he said, shocked upon hearing the news. "Man, that's really upsetting me."

And it did. He rarely shows strong emotions, but that news knocked him for a loop. I also told him about Dad, my recent existential search for answers and how I could not afford a proper diagnosis. I had found a local expert, Dr. H, who studied under Dr. Tony Attwood himself in Australia. But the price was beyond what I could afford or save up in a short period of time. It was eating at me. I had to know.

Since we were in the Park Avenue area, we went for bagels and agreed to meet back at my place afterwards. He told me he would see me there but had to do something first.

At my apartment we smoked cigars out on my balcony.

Soon after he left he texted me and told me to look between two specific titles on my bookcase. He had left me the money to see the doctor.

I can't accept this, I texted back with a lump in my throat.

Don't you dare not take it! You have to know. Now go find out, he wrote back.

So I made the appointment. Dr. H sent me several questionnaires and a list of things to do, that included having a close friend or relative write an essay about me and answer some questions. I had The Weasel do it, and he was glad to help, but only if he could correspond directly with Dr. H, which I told him how to do.

So on a sunny September morning in 2014 I went to her office on Belanger Street. Nervous beyond belief, I arrived almost an hour early, and walked around the neighbourhood contemplating what I was doing.

What if I don't have it? What a waste of my friend's money! And if it's not this, then what is it? Would I have to start all over again? What a fool I am! I'm wasting my time, my friend's money, everything!

Then I thought about the recent lunch I had with an ex-girlfriend named Isa. Despite splitting up more than a decade earlier, we still get together for lunch or dinner once or twice a year. I always feel indebted to her because we started seeing each other after we were both involved in bad relationships. Our exes were abusive, hers physically and mine verbally and emotionally. Isa was a welcome break, and always stood up for me. She made me feel like I was worth fighting for.

"You know, I have never met anyone like you," she said. "Ever. People either love you or hate you. And the ones who love you *really* love you and the ones who hate you *really* hate you. Why is that?"

Maybe today that mystery will be solved?

It was the first time I met with Dr. H face to face after exchanging numerous emails. Her office did not have a receptionist.

What the hell do her and her partners do with all the money we patients pay them?

I sat in a room with one other person waiting quietly for another psychologist.

What does she have? She looks fine. What could it be?

It was different from when I waited to see Dr. G at the Royal Vic Psychiatry department. The people in that waiting room looked, well, they looked like they belonged there. I certainly didn't feel like I did. I remember one, an older Greek man in fact, who stared at me almost angrily in the waiting room. After a while he asked me in Greek (how did he know?) what I was doing there and if I was waiting for someone receiving treatment.

"No, I'm waiting to see a doctor," I said.

"Well," he said, looking me over with his skewed eyes "you don't look like you need help."

"Thanks," I said.

Dr. H soon saw me and we began the session. She told me The Weasel had specifically asked her not to show me what he wrote in his essay. I understood. He was probably brutal. Incredibly forthright. As if he had been waiting through years of built-up frustration. But he had to be and I appreciated that. What she did tell me was that he wrote that I was "very direct and very honest."

True.

We spoke for a few more minutes. Then she said unexpectedly said: "There are 50 characteristics associated with Asperger's Syndrome. You have 44 of them. Congratulations, you're an Aspie!"

I didn't know what to say. Or how to feel.

Is this what it had been all along? Is this the answer I have been looking for?

I told her how I didn't feel like a part of my own family, and how girlfriends always break up with me mostly claiming that they didn't feel like I cared about them or the relationship.

"That's quite typical," Dr. H said, "I have a patient who is Chinese, and he once said that he never felt like he was Chinese. As for relationships, yes, partners of Aspies can feel alienated sometimes."

We talked for a little while longer, and she reassured me that it was not a terrible tragedy. That I should be happy now that I was aware.

I lumbered out of her office, not sure what to make of what just happened. I had to accept this. The more I thought about, the more the pieces of my life started falling into place. I understood myself and my actions, and slowly I assembled the parts that explained why everything in my life unfolded the way it did. It was an emotional downpour. All the times others made me feel bad about myself because I was not like them. All the failed relationships. All the missed opportunities. Every time someone came up to me angrily and admonished me for committing the horrid, unforgivable crime of speaking a little too loud, or violating some minor rule of protocol. Every time I failed to connect. Every time a girlfriend told me that I didn't care, when I did care! I cared a lot! And being an Aspie, you remember them all. Each and every last one. In detail.

Then it happened. Sitting in my car I started to feel like a weight was being lifted from my shoulders; like the chains that I have been dragging around like Jacob Marley were suddenly not there; like a burden I should never have borne had begun to gradually lift like a fog slowly penetrated by sunlight; like I had been reborn. I felt better. I finally understood everything.

Not long afterward two friends of mine, Nicholas and Geneviève, a couple I have known since college, asked me to take care of their adult son's cat for a few days. When they dropped off the feline, they asked me if I had any news of a diagnosis (I had spoken with them about this a few months earlier).

"Yes," I said, "I have it. I'm not sure what I'm going to do now."

"What do you mean?" Geneviève said. "You have had it your whole life and you don't seem that bad off. You have a university degree. A job. A car. A nice apartment. You've dated a lot of women. We met some of them; they were all really nice. And they were really pretty too, all of them. You're talented and smart. You're a good person. You have good friends. What difference should this make in your life?"

That hit me harder than a truck late for a delivery. She was right.

I'm still Andreas. Why should this change anything for the negative?

Soon I started reading more books about autism, including *Neurotribes* by Steve Silberman and *In a Different Key* by Caren Zucker and John Donvan. And I realized I had no reason to be ashamed.

Aspie's are different. And in some ways we have unique capabilities; misunderstood geniuses like Seven of Nine, Mr. Data, Mr. Spock or the X-Men. Some, like Albert Einstein, Henry Cavendish, Nikola Tesla and Thomas Edison (although none of them were ever officially diagnosed), have changed the world!

Congratulations?

Yes. Congratulations *are* in order.

* * *

When I was four and my brother was seven our parents bought us two brand new red CCM bicycles. We rode them up and down Birnam Street as often as we could. By mid-summer, it was decided that we should learn to ride without the help of the training wheels, so all four of us packed the bikes in the trunk of my dad's car and on a clear and bright Sunday afternoon we drove out to a large parking lot in a West Island industrial area.

With a pair of vise-grips Dad removed the wheels to Peter's bike first, and offered to hold the seat as he rode but my brother, always one to fly solo, said he wanted to try it on his own.

Peter launched himself and quickly controlled the bicycle like a natural. Soon enough he was doing figure-eights and had mastered the self-propelled vehicle like a pro.

Then it was my turn. I was nervous. I was scared. I feared falling and hurting myself.

"I don't want to do this," I said, whining. "Why do I have to?"

"Ahh," Dad said, "you can't use *éfta* all your life. You have to do *eet* sooner or later. *Mi fovasé.* ['Fear not.'] I will be right behind you holding your seat until you are ready."

"Okay," I said, still dreading possible personal injury.

I started pedalling slowly.

"Are you still there?" I asked.

"*Nai*," Dad answered, "*Ellah, ellah*! ['Come on, come on!'] Keep going."

So I kept pedalling until I made it across the parking lot and stopped at the edge of the curb. I turned around to find Mom, Dad and Peter all the way at the other end, waving and smiling broadly. Dad had let go after only a few steps. He was pretty astute for someone who had never owned a bicycle as a child, and never rode one in his life.

"Now come back to us," Dad said. "*Ellah piso* ['Come back'], you can do *eet*!"

And I did. I rode all the way back by myself.

We practiced in the lot for about another half hour, then loaded the bikes to go home.

During the drive I asked: "What are you going to do with the old training wheels?"

"I'm going to make a bicycle for your mother," he said, joking. And then: "You know I forget the wheels ... left them behind."

"We have to go back and get them!" I said in a panic.

"*Yeti toh thelis*?" ['Why do you want those things?'] Dad said. "Ahh! You don't need them anymore."

Acknowledgements

Every book is a collaborative effort. For their help, advice, friendship, love, and/or support, and for seeing in me something that no one else sees (that I'm still not fully convinced is there) I would like to humbly and sincerely thank (in no particular order): Kelly Norah Drukker, Mom and Dad, Peter Kessaris, Anthony Kessaris and the Kessaris and Antginas families; Michael Mirolla, Connie Guzzo McParland, Anna van Valkenburg and everyone at Guernica Editions and MiroLand; Peter Mandelos and everyone at Librairie Paragraphe Bookstore, Groupe Archambault and Renaud-Bray; Jacques Filippi, Richard King, Tommy Schnurmacher, Cora Siré, Douglas Gibson and Elise Moser; Lori Schubert and everyone at The Quebec Writers' Federation; Sharman Yarnell, Esteban Vargas and everyone at Curtains Up!; Erika Eriksson Ciment and Michel Choquette (for being like a second set of parents to me), Michele Ciment-Woods, Richard Weston, Bram Eisenthal, Rosalie Fisher, Saul Pincus and Alison MacAlpine and the Pincus family; Audrée Wilhelmy, Rafael Chimicatti, Karoline Georges, Isabelle Proulx, Lesley Salter, and Rita Schaffer; Geneviève Roy and Nicolas Bilodeau and the Roy and Bilodeau families and everyone at CFCD, Dawson College and Concordia University; Nikolas Klimis and Natalie Boky and the Klimis and Boky families; Spiros Gravas, Christos Papadatos, John Anastasopoulos, and Jerry Pimentel; the late Marc Gervais, Hillary Mashal, and Philippe Bisson (your friendships will never be forgotten).

About the Author

Andreas Kessaris grew up in Montreal's Park Extension district, the son of Greek immigrants. He is a graduate of Concordia University, where he earned a BA in Communications & English. His column, *Read On! with Andreas Kessaris* was a popular feature in the West End community paper *The Local Seeker*. His writing has also appeared on Suite101.com, in the literary journal *The Write Place*, and on the Montreal entertainment website Curtainsup.tv. Follow him on Twitter @AKessaris or Instagram www.instagram.com/andreas_kessaris/.

This book is made of paper from well-managed FSC® - certified
forests, recycled materials, and other controlled sources.